Alec Birri served thirty years with the UK Armed Forces. He commanded an operational unit that experimented in new military capabilities classified at the highest level (Top Secret Strap 3) and it is this that forms the basis of his novels.

Although semi-autobiographical, for national security and personal liberty reasons, the events and individuals portrayed have to be fiction, but are still nonetheless in keeping with his experiences.

www.alecbirri.com

CONDITION

BOOK THREE

ALEC BIRRI

Copyright © 2017 Alec Birri

The moral right of the author has been asserted.

Apart from any fair dealing for the purposes of research or private study, or criticism or review, as permitted under the Copyright, Designs and Patents Act 1988, this publication may only be reproduced, stored or transmitted, in any form or by any means, with the prior permission in writing of the publishers, or in the case of reprographic reproduction in accordance with the terms of licences issued by the Copyright Licensing Agency. Enquiries concerning reproduction outside those terms should be sent to the publishers.

Matador
9 Priory Business Park,
Wistow Road, Kibworth Beauchamp,
Leicestershire, LE8 0RX
Tel: (+44) 116 279 2299
Fax: (+44) 116 279 2277
Email: books@troubador.co.uk
Web: www.troubador.co.uk/matador

ISBN 978 1788033 190

British Library Cataloguing in Publication Data.
A catalogue record for this book is available from the British Library.

Printed and bound by CPI Group (UK) Ltd, Croydon, CR0 4YY
Typeset in 11pt Aldine by Troubador Publishing Ltd, Leicester, UK

Matador is an imprint of Troubador Publishing Ltd

Interworld /,intə'wuhld/ *n* **1** a world existing between this world and the next **2** a computer-generated environment for the use of disembodied intelligence (e.g. humans, Apals, Acarers, Aservants, etc.) capable of merging (telepathy).

PROLOGUE

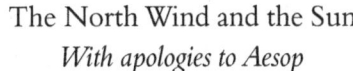

The North Wind and the Sun
With apologies to Aesop

'Go on, then.'

'Don't be ridiculous.'

'What's the matter? Anyone would think you were scared.'

'That's equally nonsensical – I'm a celestial body, and you are a by-product of my activity. The very idea of entering into competition with each other is laughable.'

The North Wind looked at the Sun and then at the man walking on the Earth's surface below. He puffed at the man's cloak and it flapped open.

'Tell you what. I'll shift some of these clouds out of the way to give you a fighting chance. What could be fairer than that?'

The Sun sighed. 'The only reason you can even do that is because of me. You're nothing more than an aspect of the weather. You might as well challenge the rain to a race.'

'I did – and the snow, too. But the harder I blew, the faster we all went. Dead heat every time. Thunder and lightning were the same, just more dramatic.'

'Yes, I've noticed you've all become more active recently. You do realise the occupants of this planet have to put up with the damage you cause?'

The man appeared about to undo the clasp on his cloak, so the North Wind moved the clouds back again. 'Well, what do you expect? Forget *your* activity; if it wasn't for man's, the weather wouldn't be getting stronger and keen to prove it. If you have a problem with that, then it's human beings you should be blaming, not us.'

The clouds evaporated. The breeze was picked up in response.

'Are you saying *man* can influence you more than I can?'

'What other explanation could there be? In some parts of the world the rain has never been heavier, the snow deeper or storms more violent – I can exceed well over 200 miles per hour these days and all thanks to man.'

The Sun reflected on its activity. The man with the cloak would be experiencing the latest effects of solar radiation in a little over eight minutes. 'So, let me get this right. You think a creature that, in cosmological terms, has existed for less than a blink of an eye is more powerful than the force that created it?'

'And you say *I'm* being ridiculous. It's got nothing to do with who's stronger. You may have spent billions of years producing life here, but it's all finely balanced. You're too slow – in *a blink of an eye* man has changed the environment for the worse, but if it's going to take you billions of years to fix, who's the more powerful?'

The North Wind blew harder. To its annoyance, the man responded by pulling the cloak around him. Seven minutes before it would be removed by other means.

'More nonsense, Wind. When it comes to the weather, Water and I have an excellent relationship and have done for the last four billion years – whatever you or your friends decide to do will be balanced out somewhere else. We might be slow, but we're not stupid.'

'But what are you going to do when that's no longer possible?' The North Wind increased the breeze to a gale. It affected the man's progress but not the grip on his cloak.

Six minutes.

'What do you mean?' said the Sun.

'Man-made greenhouse gases. No managing the effect of those by shifting the problem elsewhere – unless you consider turning arable lands into deserts fair compensation for melting icecaps – you're going to have to reduce your output.'

'That won't be happening anytime soon, and anyway, it's not as if we haven't been here before. Life on the Earth is constantly evolving and has done since the beginning of time.' The Sun looked at the other planets in its solar system. 'A healthy balance between Water and me would appear to be essential, I grant you, but even if humans were to find themselves unable to exist, there are plenty of other creatures happy to take their place and if there aren't, natural selection will soon produce some – look what happened after the dinosaurs.'

Five minutes. The sky was now cloudless, but the speed of the gale and the direction it came from ensured the last thing the man wanted to do was sunbathe. He pulled the cloak even tighter. The North Wind tutted to itself.

'But that was caused by something out of the dinosaurs' control. What's happening now is unique in the Earth's history; one of its species is wiping itself out and taking all the other animals and plants with it.'

Four minutes. The strength of the gale was increased to force nine which caused trees to shed their branches. The man gave up on his journey but not on his cloak. Much to the North Wind's chagrin, the man sat in the lee of a rock and held the two halves of it together.

'Well, that's the beauty of nature,' said the Sun. 'You never know what you're going to get. Who knows, maybe in as little as a hundred thousand years a new species will spring up out of nowhere and with an ability to correct everything man's done wrong.'

'*A hundred thousand years?* Look around. Human beings have irreparably damaged the atmosphere in less than a century. I told you, you're too slow. Pretty soon both the air and water will be so toxic, nothing nature can produce will be able to survive. It'll be like going back to when the Earth first formed.'

Three minutes and gale force ten. The trees stopped losing their branches but only because they were being uprooted.

'Is that what you're saying?' said the Sun. 'Man is so powerful, he can not only end his own existence and the life of every creature and plant but even *evolution* itself?'

Two minutes. The gale was now a storm, but the man managed to hold on to both himself and the cloak. The North Wind considered producing a hurricane but guessed that would end in blowing the man and his cloak away together. It gave up.

One minute.

The man peered from behind the rock. He'd never known weather like it – a raging tempest one second and dead calm the next. Maybe he was in the eye of the storm?

He stood up to survey the scene while he thought he still could. The detritus of uprooted trees and branches lay all around. It was a miracle he hadn't been struck by one of them – mayhem as far as the eye could see. He smiled at the Sun's reassuring presence before reaching up to his neck. It would be the last conscious thing he would do.

At tens of thousands of degrees Fahrenheit and a speed of over 500 miles per second, he would never know whether it was the solar flare's heat that finally removed his cloak – or its blast.

PART ONE

2028

CHAPTER ONE

The noise of the motorcycle's engine rebounded off the sides of the wadi.

'Where are we going?'

'You'll soon find out.'

'But, Baba, we've been in the desert for hours. Mama will be worried.'

'She knows where we're going, and stop exaggerating – it's been forty minutes at most.'

Isra winced at every rut and loose rock. Sitting astride the machine would be a relief but even suggesting it would result in the back of her father's hand.

'I feel sick.'

'For the love of God, Isra, will you just shut up? We have to be at the rendezvous before sunset.'

'Baba, please stop. I'm going to be sick – I have to take my pill anyway.'

'Another twenty minutes won't make any difference. You'll just have to hold—' Vomit ran down Faruk's back. His daughter threw herself to the ground the moment the motorcycle came to a halt. 'Allah give me strength! You're supposed to be getting better – not worse.' He reached into a bag.

Isra wiped a hand across her mouth before grabbing what was being held out.

'You are the most ungrateful child it has ever been my misfortune to have, and if it weren't for the wishes of The Prophet – peace be upon him – I would leave you here right now.'

It didn't take long for the red pill to do its work. *Prophet? Wishes?* Isra got up and squinted in the direction they were heading. The setting sun made it difficult to see but other than the odd dust devil there was nothing for miles. She zoomed her new eyesight onto the horizon but that just magnified the haze. 'Why didn't you say?'

Faruk scowled. 'Because you're the kind of child that already thinks they're something special and the thought of you being chosen to do God's work too can only make the rest of us wish you hadn't been.'

She squared up to him. 'I'm not a child, I'm thirteen – a woman.'

Faruk remounted the motorbike. 'You're a woman when I say you are – get on.'

Their journey continued, but Isra was no longer concerned with the comfort of it. 'What does he want me for?'

She didn't get an answer.

'It must be something very important.' Isra tried playing down the honour of being chosen by The Prophet. 'Whatever it is, I will carry it out to the best of my ability – Allah's will must be done.' She recited a prayer before allowing excitement to get the better of her. 'For God to return The Prophet to Earth is one thing but to be actually chosen by him…' She stared into space. 'Maybe he wants me for his wife?' She cringed at the thought. 'He's very old, though.' Her face brightened up again. 'But he can do anything so maybe he'll appear to me as a younger man? Either way, if The Prophet needs me for his wife then so be it,' she conjected on the outcome. 'I wonder how many children he wants? The boys will all have to come first, of course, but they're going to look very strange.' Isra prodded her father in the back. 'Baba, why do you think Allah did it?'

'Did what?'

'The Prophet. Why did God choose to return him as a white man?'

The motorcycle came to a stop again, and Isra prepared herself for another scolding – or something worse. She raised an arm just in case. She dropped it when her father didn't say or do anything. He was looking at the cloud of dust approaching them from the other direction. Faruk switched off the engine.

The Honda pulled up alongside, and its rider did the same. He looked at Isra. She covered her face.

'Is this the girl?' Faruk nodded. 'Follow me.'

The stranger turned his vehicle through ninety degrees and set off in a new direction. There was an AK47 strapped to his back.

The sight of a rifle wasn't unusual in this part of the world, but the man's foreign accent was. Isra whispered, 'Mujahid.' Faruk ran a hand over his greying beard as if trying to take in the significance. He kicked the motorcycle back into life.

CHAPTER TWO

It was dusk when they arrived. A Bedouin tent in the middle of nowhere. Not unusual but not what Faruk was expecting, especially given the number of vehicles and people he could see standing outside. A curious mix of animals too – camels, donkeys and even horses stood tethered to four-by-fours and pickup trucks.

Others were arriving at the same time, which helped Faruk with his need to be inconspicuous, but not with his nerves. Especially once the people could be identified; the four-legged creatures present might have been content to socialise but not all of the two-legged. Faruk spat on the ground.

'Leave the girl here.'

'What? With these murderers and rapists?'

Their guide tilted his head up. 'The Great Satan is less likely to strike where women and children can be seen.'

Faruk now realised there weren't just Shia men to take offence at – some of their women and children were present too. To his further disgust, they were socialising with his own people. 'What is the meaning of this insult to God?'

The guide placed a hand on the butt of his AK47. 'You're not here to ask questions. She'll be safe with them.' Faruk looked in the direction the man was pointing. A group of toothless crones smiled back.

'Go to those women, Isra.'

'But I don't know them.'

'Don't argue.' Faruk grabbed his daughter's arm as she dismounted the motorbike. 'And keep away from *them*.' Isra promised.

Faruk was led to the tent's entrance where he baulked at the white face of the man who wanted to search him. '*American?*'

The man shook his head and passed a detector over Faruk's body. 'Chechen.'

'*Russian?*'

The man shook his head again. 'No, *Chechen*.' He retained Faruk's mobile phone.

Faruk didn't know what to make of him. Having said that, he didn't know what to make of his guide either. Too late to back out now.

He was encouraged to enter the tent alone. It was like stepping into a palace. Not that Faruk had ever had the pleasure. A sumptuous luxury of deep-pile rugs, silk-lined drapes and intricately designed lanterns made one thing clear – this was no ordinary command post.

The uncomfortable blend of nationalities and loyalties extended into here too. The only difference was social standing. High-ranking Imams and Clerics of dubious faiths mixed with influential businessmen and other privileged individuals. Inadequacy joined Faruk's trepidation.

A woman approached with her head bowed. She carried a tray of drinks that Faruk neither recognised nor trusted. He shook his head. She then met his gaze, and he realised it wasn't a woman at all. The lifeless eyes of a robot stared back.

Could anything be more offensive?

'Welcome!'

A man dressed in a traditional Saudi thawb and headdress appeared.

'My name is Prince Ali Bin Hassan. And you must be Far—'

Faruk reacted as if his past had finally caught up with him – he fell to his knees. 'Your Royal Highness – please. Forgive me – I beg of you!' A series of confessions followed as if to lessen the degree of punishment Faruk was now expecting. The prince interrupted them.

'Peace be upon you, my brother.'

Faruk lifted his head and stared at the hand being offered. He then realised others in the tent were regarding him in the same quizzical way.

'Please, all are welcome here.'

Foolishness became Faruk's only emotion. He took the prince's hand – the grubbiness of Faruk's own caused him some embarrassment. He got back to his feet.

'Yes, I should imagine it must seem strange if not actually shocking to see so many of our brothers here.'

Faruk still had contempt for some of those around him. 'Brothers?'

'Well, let us be polite and use the word "associates". Either way, now that *Yawn ad-Din* is nearly upon us, it's only right that we should form an alliance before the battle begins.'

The Aservant offered Hassan the same tray of refreshments. Faruk sniffed the mixture of water and fruit juice before taking a sip. 'The Day of Judgement is near?'

'Of course, or did you think The Prophet – peace be upon him – returned just to cure your daughter's blindness?' Faruk asked again for his blasphemy to be forgiven, but Hassan didn't deem it necessary. 'How is Isra? How's your family coping with the other blessings bestowed upon her?'

Faruk was keen not to cause offence, but his disappointment with the miracle couldn't be hidden. 'We are indeed grateful for the return of her sight, Your Royal Highness, but it is as if The Devil himself is determined to have his say. Before the blessings, and despite her blindness, Isra was a good, hard-working girl who obeyed her mother and prayed five times a day. But now it is as though her mind is fighting a possess—' He stopped himself for fear of sounding ungrateful to God.

Hassan empathised. 'I know the difficulties you're going through, my friend. As a father of seventeen myself, I too found the freeing of their thoughts difficult to understand, but once I'd received the same blessing everything became clear.' He clicked his fingers. The Aservant approached again but this time with a silver platter. A small, carved wooden box sat in the middle and Hassan lifted the lid. 'The mission Isra and you have to undertake will require a similar clarity of mind.'

A red pill lay on a silk cushion. This pill was different to the capsules Faruk had seen his daughter take – larger, and more transparent. Something moved. He leaned forward in case it was a trick of the light and was struck by turmoil. The red liquid inside clawed at the interior of the tablet as if desperate for an escape.

Faruk stood back. 'Isra *and* me?'

'Of course.'

'But I'm a simple farmer. What could The Prophet – peace be upon him – possibly want with me?'

Hassan closed the lid and put the box in Faruk's hand.

'We both know the answer to that.'

CHAPTER THREE

'I told you to stay away from them!'

Faruk grabbed Isra's arm and threw her to the ground. He raised a hand to strike his daughter, but found himself unable to do so. His eyes met those of the men who had intervened. Faruk's feet left the ground as he was then placed out of harm's way.

'Clarity of mind, my brother.' The prince stepped over Faruk before assisting his daughter to her feet. 'A father's need to protect his family's honour is indeed important, but the victory of our people far more so and you must concentrate on that.' He pointed at the box still in Faruk's hand.

Hassan signalled towards the car park, where a set of headlights came on. A Toyota SUV left the menagerie of other vehicles and pulled up alongside him. One of Hassan's men went to open a door but stepped aside when the prince himself invited Isra to enter. She looked at her father. He nodded.

Isra bowed her head and was about to climb in when the prince appeared to have a change of heart. 'You are required to look to the skies, Isra.' He paused before adding, 'Forgive the impertinence but I'm afraid your head must first be uncovered.'

Isra looked again to her father for guidance and he was about to protest, when all the men in the vicinity turned their backs on his daughter. Even the prince had averted his eyes. What made this action stranger was the way in which it was done – synchronised, as if all were of one mind. Faruk indicated for his daughter to get on with it.

The Aservant seemed content with the glance Isra gave the heavens and assisted in redressing the hijab. It got into the vehicle with her. Faruk grabbed his bag, put the box into it and got to his feet. He was about to enter the Toyota when the prince stopped him too. 'The Prophet – peace be upon him – requires you to do the same, my brother.'

Faruk hesitated but then pulled down his own headdress, tilted his chin up for a second and got into the front of the vehicle. The white face of its driver didn't surprise him as much this time.

'Chechen?'

'Nae, pal – Scottish.'

'*British?*'

'Why don't you call me English and really upset me?'

Laughter made Faruk turn round.

'Times are changing, my friend – as you will soon find out.' Hassan bade them a traditional Saudi farewell and the vehicle moved off.

Faruk turned to check on his daughter. The robot was staring straight ahead, but Isra wasn't. Faruk skewed the rear-view mirror more towards the handsome young driver who stopped grinning when faced with his own reflection. He put out a hand.

'Mohammed – call me Mo.'

Faruk blanked the gesture. 'You Westerners.'

'What about us?'

Faruk ignored that too. 'And where exactly is *Mo* from in Scotland?'

'Glasgow. Does it matter?'

'You think to become a Muslim all one need do is take on the most sacred name, insult it, read the Koran and say your prayers when you want to – you know nothing.'

'Oh, I don't know. The reason I became a Muslim in the first place was because The Prophet spoke to me.'

'The Prophet – peace be upon him – spoke to *you?*'

'Yeah, when I was in prison. Took one of those pills, and that was it – couldn't be clearer.'

The admission didn't exactly warm Faruk to his new companion. 'And just when did this miracle happen?'

'Ooh. Must be six months now.'

'Six months? You think six months of good words and deeds is enough to ensure God's forgiveness?' He turned away in disgust. 'If the day of reckoning is truly here, then you will soon be crossing the bridge with the rest of us and the weight of your sins will carry you to where you belong – *infidel.*'

Mo moved the mirror back and winked at Isra. Her eyes betrayed a hidden smile. 'Look, there's a good six hours ahead of us. The least we can do is be nice to each other.'

Six hours. Faruk studied the map on the vehicle's heads-up display. He voiced concerns with the route. 'Levant. That's part of the Caliphate's empire.'

'And?'

'If we're stopped, they'll kill you, and punish us.'

'Why would they do that?'

Faruk glanced over his shoulder at Isra. 'Because you're an infidel, of course!'

'Nonsense. You don't have a monopoly on what makes a good Muslim.'

'For all our sakes, we must go around.'

'Don't worry, everything will be fine – the route's being protected.' Mo winked at Isra's reflection again before letting go of the steering wheel and raising both hands. 'Allah's will must be done!'

Faruk grimaced. 'We'd better stop before we cross the border – it might be the last chance we get.'

'Last chance for what?'

Faruk stared at Mo. 'If you don't know, then that proves what you are, *infidel*.' Faruk pretended to spit.

Mo shrugged with exasperation. 'Okay, okay, but let's get some sand under us first.'

Two hours later and the satnav indicated a border village would be visible from the next ridge. Mo brought the SUV to a stop just before it. They all exited the vehicle and were soon peering down on a jungle of light sources in the valley below.

'Any Caliphate flags or markings?'

Isra magnified the scene. 'It's too dark to see anything but street lamps, Baba.'

Faruk turned to Mo. 'Do your weapons have night sights?'

'Weapons?'

'Yes, the weapons needed to protect my daughter and me during our journey.'

'I've already told you – Allah's protecting us.'

Faruk approached Mo. 'You plan to take us through the Levant with *nothing*?'

'Of course not – there's a cool box.'

Faruk went to grab Mo, but he was too quick for him and had stepped to one side. Faruk found himself scrabbling in the sand instead. He got back up to have another go at teaching the young man a lesson, but thought better of it.

Mo raised his eyebrows at Faruk before turning to Isra. 'Try filtering out the streetlights first and then intensifying what's in between. Use infra-red if you have to.' Father and daughter regarded Mo as if he were speaking a foreign language. 'It's no different to filtering out the noise of other people's thoughts. I can show you if you like?' Faruk glowered at Mo. 'Er, it might be better if your companion robot did.'

The Aservant turned to Isra and, in an instant, her expression went from puzzlement to understanding. She gazed back down to the village and grinned.

'No flags, Baba, but there are markings. *Revolution is coming; Death to non-believers; Jihad to America; Allah is greatest...*' She trailed off when she realised her father was looking at her in the same way he did Mo.

'How long have you been able to read?' His daughter didn't reply. The robot moved between the two of them.

Faruk forced himself to remain calm. 'It's time to pray.'

He was about to open his bag when Isra, Mo and the robot turned their heads in a new direction. They opened their mouths to say something, but it was Isra who spoke.

'We must get back into the vehicle, Baba. *Now*.' Mo indicated there was no time to explain – by frogmarching Faruk towards it.

Faruk strained to see what was so important that his servitude to God had to be interrupted. 'What is it? What can you see?'

'We don't know, Baba. But it's coming this way.'

Faruk couldn't see or hear anything. They got back into the Toyota, and the four of them continued staring into the darkness, but Faruk had soon given up. He took a moment to study the faces that were clearly absorbing the increasing detail of whatever it was. The robot remained expressionless, but Isra and Mo's mouths moved together in silence as if providing a running commentary for lip-readers. Faruk couldn't help thinking, but for that, they appeared no different to the Aservant.

They stopped. The three then faced Faruk. 'We must pray now, Baba.'

Faruk stared at his daughter as she closed her eyes and did just that. Mo and the robot were doing the same. Faruk was about to join them when the Toyota's interior was illuminated by a bright light.

'US ARMY. GET OUT OF THE VEHICLE.'

Faruk squinted in the direction of both the floodlight and the Arabic coming out of a loudspeaker.

'GET OUT OF THE VEHICLE OR WE'LL BE FORCED TO OPEN FIRE.'

Faruk went to comply, but Mo had taken his arm. He didn't open his eyes and said, 'You must stay with us, my brother.'

There was movement beyond Mo – the GIs had dismounted their vehicles and were closing in on foot. Silhouettes made it clear where rifles were pointing. Faruk implored his driver, 'We must do what the Americans say.'

Mo kept his eyes shut. 'No, my brother. We must do what *God* says.'

The first one died in silence – the thickness of the Toyota's windows and shrapnel-proof construction ensuring Faruk only saw and didn't hear the body separating into three pieces. Even the dull thud of its torso landing on the bonnet went unnoticed. What scythed through the rest of the soldiers went about its business just as quietly – until the cannon shells began impacting on the border patrol's vehicles.

Unlike sand or flesh, the armour was hard enough to detonate the small charge within the centre of each munition, and although the floodlight had now ceased to function, flashes from hundreds of tiny but deadly explosions lit up enough of the scene to see what was going on. Even a billowing cloud of dust and smoke couldn't hide it. Despite blast-waves slamming the Toyota, Faruk closed his eyes, covered his ears and tried not to be sick, while praying for his daughter's life.

CHAPTER FOUR

Mo punched the air. '*Allahu Akbar!* God is greatest!' He opened the Toyota's door and fell over the lump of flesh lying on the ground beside it. Scrambling to his feet, he switched on his night vision. A bloom of infra-red from vehicle fires and the occasional round cooking-off couldn't mask a heat-haze of cooling body parts. He turned back to Faruk.

'What did I tell you?! God is truly the greatest! Who needs weapons when Allah himself is watching over you? Who needs an army when—'

Faruk was staring straight ahead but not very far – the recognisable parts of a GI were staring back at him through the windshield. Mo rushed to drag the torso from the pickup's hood. He tried enthusing his passenger again.

'Who needs an army when – oh, *fuck*.' Mo ran around the vehicle, checking each corner of it. 'Fuck, fuck, fuck.' The Toyota's armoured body may have been able to withstand the blast fragments but not its tyres. Mo took out his mobile phone. He swore again. 'We're going to have to—' He cut himself off once more when he realised Isra was sobbing. The robot had its arm around her.

Mo opened the door and leaned in. 'Are you okay?'

Isra didn't answer. Her head was down, and she was shaking.

'Of course she's not *okay*.' If Faruk was in shock too, he didn't show it. He put his hand on his daughter's knee, but she brushed it away.

'I'm afraid the pickup's had it, and there's no signal here,' said Mo. 'We're going to have to enter the village on foot.' He put a hand out to Isra but withdrew it when he saw the look on her father's face. The Aservant encouraged Isra out of the Toyota instead and guided her through the detritus of body parts. Mo and Faruk grabbed their belongings and followed.

'What do we do now?' said Faruk.

'Find a signal and report what's happened.' Mo hoped he sounded reassuring. 'Don't worry, God will soon have us on our way again.'

Faruk kept a distance but was close enough to see his daughter's gradual recovery from the ordeal. By the time they reached the outskirts of the village, she no longer needed the robot's support, and was looking for something in the distance.

Faruk caught up. 'What is it, Isra?'

'What time is it, Baba?'

He looked at his watch. 'Just before ten.'

She stopped. 'Then where is everybody?'

Mo and the robot stood next to Isra and all three stared down the street ahead. It was lit well enough for

Faruk to do the same but he had soon exhausted his visual method of checking for signs of life.

'Well?'

'Nothing, Baba. No people, no animals – nothing.'

The Aservant turned to Mo, who sniffed the air in response. 'There is something.' Mo looked back at the robot as if to confirm the assessment. '*Death.*'

Faruk was about to challenge that when the previously unnoticed background hum of electricity generators became a concern – the change in tone as one of them ran down was accompanied by that part of the village descending into darkness.

Mo reached into his backpack and gave Faruk a torch. 'Just in case we get split up.' They headed down the street.

Mo took out his phone again but was soon shaking his head. 'We might need sat-comms instead. There's bound to be a GPS transceiver somewhere – the village looks big enough.'

They reached a junction, and the Aservant stopped. It then turned to face a new direction and began walking again. It wasn't long before even Faruk could see the reason why – the source of what the robot had first sensed on entering the village: Death. What appeared to be the town's entire complement of livestock lay motionless in the middle of the market square, as many as a hundred goats and a similar number of sheep.

At first glance, none had suffered any trauma and what made that more unusual was the healthy state of the cadavers – they could almost have been asleep.

The robot got on its hands and knees and sniffed at one of the dead animals. 'An overdose of barbiturates. Administered less than twelve hours ago.'

Three of the visitors looked up. 'Listen. Can you hear it?' said Isra. 'People are praying.' All four moved to where she was pointing.

It wasn't long before Faruk could hear it too. 'A funeral prayer.' He made for the mosque but soon realised that that wasn't where the chanting was coming from. He followed the others to where it was – a small and less impressive building in the next street. No sooner had they got there than Faruk realised similar prayers could be heard coming from the house next door. And the one across the street from that. Electric lighting still bathed this part of the village but the properties themselves were in darkness. Faruk knocked on a door. No answer. He rapped it again before switching on the torch and entering the house – just as the street faded to black when a second generator ran out of fuel.

Seeing the whole family in one room wasn't unusual, but the nature of their condition was. All of them – three adults and six children of varying ages – lay on the ground curled up like foetuses. Each was wrapped in a white linen cloth and facing the same direction. One of the children held a kitten – just as lifeless as its owner.

The prayers were being generated by an old tape player, but without mains electricity its batteries soon strained. Faruk switched the player off before closing his eyes and replacing it with a prayer of his own. Curiosity ended it early. 'What happened here? Were they struck by an illness?'

The robot inspected one of the cadavers in the same way it had the sheep. It then placed a finger against the child's temple. 'Another sedative overdose, but not long ago – the body's temperature is 80.4 degrees Fahrenheit.'

Faruk shone his torch across the family, but then realised a faint glow could be seen emanating from within each shroud. He peeled away part of the largest body's covering – it was holding an iPad.

Faruk prised the tablet from the cadaver's hands. 'A home movie. The whole family, by the look of it.' Faruk scanned them again. Each was holding a similar device. 'They must have known their time was at an end and wanted to die with their happiest memories.'

Mo looked over Faruk's shoulder. 'It's not a recording.' Another of the village's electricity generators coughed. 'We'd better find some comms before all the power goes.'

'What do you mean, "It's not a recording"?'

Mo didn't respond to Faruk's question and followed the robot outside. Faruk was about to return the tablet to the body's hands when something on the screen made him stop. He brought it up to his face.

It was clearly a joyous occasion. The entire family less the father, and Faruk assumed him to be the cameraman. Everyone was smiling, laughing, embracing – even the kitten was receiving its fair share of hugs. Faruk realised the event had taken place in the very same room he and his daughter were standing. It made the sight of their bodies more pitiful. He motioned for Isra to look but she shook her head as if afraid.

'Put it back, Baba.'

Her father was about to do as asked, when he caught sight of someone else in the video – someone who wasn't now decomposing on the floor along with the rest of the family, and conspicuous by an absence of occasion. He waited for the woman to reappear and, when she did, Faruk realised it wasn't a person at all – it was a robot. The contrast between its lifeless expression and the animated gestures of the human beings in the video could not have been starker.

Faruk wondered where the family's Aservant was now and was about to search for it when the cameraman zoomed in on the android's face. It seemed to stare back at him. Not at the cameraman, but at Faruk. The robot's emotionless features were unsettling, and Faruk closed his eyes. It was as if the tablet were a portal to another world and the robot was willing him to enter it – like Azrael would when it became Faruk's time to die.

Isra turned away from the device. 'Put it back, Baba.' She left the house.

With some relief, Faruk returned the tablet to the body's hands and redressed the shroud. He then asked Allah to forgive the family their sins and went outside.

Light from Faruk's torch landed on his daughter's kneeling form and he lost his temper. 'Isra! Get out of the dirt!' He grabbed his daughter's arm, but her superior strength soon had it wrestled away again.

'You don't understand. You *never* understand!' Isra

burst into tears and ran – straight into the arms of her companion robot.

'They're in Barzakh.'

Faruk regarded Mo as if he'd taken leave of his senses. 'Barzakh? The *Interworld*? Don't be ridiculous.'

Mo didn't bother arguing and changed the subject. 'We've found a signal – God will meet us on the far side of town just before sunrise.'

Faruk was incredulous. 'May Allah have mercy on your soul – is there no end to your blasphemy?'

Mo ignored that too. He glanced in the direction he and the robot had just come from. 'We can spend the night there. I suggest we make the most of it.' He grinned. 'Meeting our maker is going to be amazing!'

Faruk was speechless. He prayed for Mo's forgiveness, but stopped when the words sank in. *Meeting our maker.*

CHAPTER FIVE

Faruk had never expected to feel sorry for Mo. 'Who did you speak to?'

The young Glaswegian took a sleeping bag out of his pack. 'The prince.'

'What did he say?'

'I told you – be on the far side of town before sunrise.'

The robot and Isra returned from checking the rest of the building. She handed her father a couple of figs. 'Ula says the water's safe to drink too, Baba. May I have one of my pills now, please?'

He gave her the bottle. '*Ula?*'

'We can't keep calling her *it* all the time. Not when she's being so helpful.'

Her? She? Faruk scowled at the robot. It offered him a biscuit. He bit into it.

Mo passed the sleeping bag to Faruk. 'It's just as frustrating for us, my brother. Everything will become clear once you've taken the pill and your mission is complete.'

Ordinarily, Faruk would get angry, but he didn't. He hadn't taken much notice of the way Mo talked before but it appeared different now somehow. Maybe Faruk was becoming accustomed to his Scottish accent?

'You do know what is meant by "meeting one's maker"?' said Faruk.

'Yes.'

'Then you'll understand why my daughter and I will be travelling on our own tomorrow.'

'How are you going to do that?' said Mo.

'There will be a vehicle somewhere. I doubt the owner will mind.'

'But you don't know where you're going.'

'The satnav made it plain enough and what happened to the Americans earlier tells me you're right about the route being protected.'

Mo exchanged looks with the robot, and it approached Faruk. 'I'm afraid you must stay with us, brother – Allah has commanded it.'

Faruk went to strike the android, but it anticipated the blow and grabbed Faruk's wrist. Faruk tried punching with his other fist, but found himself a gasping heap on the floor instead. He was about to give "Ula" a mouthful when the robot's expression reminded Faruk of the Aservant in the video. He couldn't stand this gaze for long either. Isra assisted her father to his feet and sat him in a chair. He recovered his breath and attempted to do the same with his dignity.

'As a devout Sunni Muslim I find it difficult to accept how a Westerner could possibly comprehend in a few months what it has taken my entire life to barely understand, but when I hear a *machine* blaspheming…'

Mo turned his head to one side. 'Even if your response might result in your death?'

'Then I'll have died fighting for the will of Allah and be rewarded in Heaven for it.' Faruk put a hand to a sudden migraine.

Mo knelt and offered Faruk a bottle of water. 'But it is Allah's will that we meet him, brother. If you try and stop that, then surely it is *you* who is guilty of blasphemy?'

Faruk was about to deliver short shrift again when his eyesight blurred. He blinked a couple of times to retain his view of the younger man, but it didn't seem to do any good. Faruk drank some more of the water. 'Nonsense. You don't know what you're say—'

The migraine eased just as a distant roar of the sea began. Faruk shook his head to rid himself of both annoyances, but that appeared to cause his blurred vision to distort – Mo grew taller. As did Isra. Faruk then realised they weren't growing – they were floating. Floating about a foot above the floor. He put a hand out to his daughter, but only managed to touch the tips of her fingers before she began ascending out of reach. Faruk stood up to grab her, but a stomach cramp forced him to stay seated.

He looked up – both Isra and Mo were rising towards a bright light in the centre of the ceiling. Faruk was sure if he stretched enough he would be able to reach his daughter, but the ceiling climbed away too.

'No! Don't leave me!'

He reached as far above his head as he could, but it was too late – they were being taken by the light, and there was nothing Faruk could do. Soon, they were both too far away to see, and the light had become just another star in the night.

Faruk looked around. The walls of the building had vanished. So had the village. He was standing in the middle of the desert. The vastness of both it and the heavens made him shiver. He went to sit back in the chair, but that had also disappeared. He was alone. More alone than he had ever been. Nothing. No sound, no light – nothing. Just an expanse of cold, dark solitude. He fell to his knees and cried.

'What? No prayers, Faruk?'

Faruk's head jerked back up but only to meet the eyes of the dead family's Aservant. Faruk prayed like he had never prayed before.

'Too late for that now – come with me.'

Faruk's prayers halted and he stared at the sand in front of him. The robot's words had replaced the devout man's fears with first, realisation, and then, acceptance. 'I know who you are. Azrael – the Angel of Death.' Faruk got to his feet, but still couldn't look fate in the eye. 'I am ready.'

The angel walked, and Faruk trudged after it. He peered in the direction they were heading, but it was too dark to see. Being dead didn't bother him. 'Where are we going?'

'Where do you think we're going?'

Faruk hesitated in case the answer itself would be judged, but the teachings had made it plain enough. '*As Sarat* – the bridge.'

The angel said nothing, so Faruk assumed his passage to paradise had started well. He chanted the required supplication to ensure forgiveness and guidance on the crossing. He stopped midway through it.

'Where's my daughter? Why isn't she here with me? If we're all dead, then why aren't Isra and Mo crossing the bridge too?'

'They already have.'

'But we died together.'

'Their sins were easier to judge.'

'Easier?'

'Yes, one crossed to Heaven in moments while the other fell to Hell just as quickly. Your sins are more complex.'

'*More complex?* But I've dedicated my entire life to the teachings of The Prophet – peace be upon him – and have carried out Allah's will implicitly. That cannot be ignored.'

'*Cannot be ignored?* I think the sin of arrogance just caused the bridge to grow a few more thorns for you to trip on.'

Faruk cursed to himself.

'And that expletive has resulted in the surface becoming yet more slippery.'

Faruk bit his lip and went back to the supplication. He had soon interrupted it again.

'What do you mean by "more complex"?'

'Impatience won't make the journey any easier either, Faruk, but let's examine your record, shall we?' The night sky filled with what looked to be the highs and lows of Faruk's life. 'Your first wife and child. Why did you leave them?'

'To do God's bidding, of course – fighting the Russians in Afghanistan.'

'Why didn't you return to them once the jihad was over and the Russians had been defeated?'

Faruk was on safe ground answering that question. 'The success meant a calling elsewhere – I fought Iranian infidels after that and all in God's good name.'

'Which got you captured, tortured and then released as part of a prisoner exchange. Why didn't you return to your family then?'

Faruk answered this question with the same confidence. 'Because I was now a battlefield commander and with that status came more wives. God rewards believers with children, and the greater one's belief, the more one is blessed with them.'

The angel stopped walking. 'You fought in Syria after that. What happened to the children there?'

Faruk knew what his ethereal guide was alluding to and chose to look it in the eye. It didn't bother him anymore. 'They were Christians – Allah had already decided their fate.'

'But was it necessary to behead them?'

'A message had to be sent. God's will *must* be done.'

'But some were Muslims, and you knew that.'

'They lived with the Christian infidels, and that is an abomination to God.'

'Nevertheless, they died reciting the exact same prayers as you did just now and before crossing the path you're about to take, so you can see the difficulty – Allah now has to judge a man who spent over sixty years putting God above all else and yet at the same time denied hundreds of others the very same opportunity.'

Faruk was unmoved. 'God knows everything I have done was in his name and for that alone my sins will be forgiven.'

Azrael looked down and Faruk realised they were standing on the edge of a precipice. He leaned over it. The gloom below was impossible to penetrate.

'What is this?'

'*As Sarat.*'

'But there's nothing here.'

'Look again, Faruk.'

A light appeared in the distance. It emanated with rays, one of which ran all the way to Faruk's feet. He then realised it wasn't a ray at all, but a silken thread – reflecting where he was expected to try and make for.

'But that's impossible!'

'Impossible? Are you saying you lack both the purity *and* the faith to cross it?'

Faruk glared at Azrael. 'Why have you chosen to appear to me in the form of a machine?'

'I haven't.' The light bathed the angel's features. It wasn't the dead family's Aservant after all – it was Ula.

'Ula is still a machine!'

'Should you make it across, I wonder if you will find God just as disappointing?'

Faruk turned back to the brightness. His faith was being tested – that's all. Everything would become clear once he was on the other side. He restarted the supplication, focussed on his goal and took the first step towards it.

The bridge was just as the teachings had said it would be – precarious and as slippery as ice underfoot. It even sagged with Faruk's weight, and for a moment he thought he would tumble to his doom there and then, but the slope caused him to slide to a stop instead – against what he assumed to be one of many trip hazards to be faced along the way. Faruk expected his next step to be just as unsure but the thorn that pierced his foot both pained and reassured at the same time. He was about to take another when he heard a voice calling out to him.

'Faruk! Run! Now!'

The voice came from the light. It was too bright to see, but Faruk knew who it was. He took another step but only to trip over a root that would have sent a less faithful Muslim straight to Hell. He was wondering whether to do as Mo had asked when the significance of his voice sank in.

'But that means…' The realisation caused Faruk to look down. He could see it now – a second light. Not as bright as the first, but then the flames of damnation aren't supposed to be.

'Baba? Can you hear me?'

Faruk closed his eyes. The teachings had said nothing of this. Nothing of a *choice* to be made on the bridge. He raised a fist to God. '*Why?* Why take an infidel over an innocent child? To punish me? Why punish my daughter for *my* sins?' Tears streamed down his face.

The silken thread sagged yet more until Faruk was close enough to hear the very screams of Hell, but in that instant, he no longer cared. Even when Satan himself appeared and blasted a breath of fire and brimstone straight into Faruk's face, he was left unmoved. The Devil opened his mouth, put out a tongue and invited his latest soul to step onto it.

Faruk's footing was becoming less and less secure but that no longer mattered and nor did God's judgement – Faruk would be judging himself. If his daughter had to face an eternity of unimaginable torment, then so would he. Staring down the throat of the monster, Faruk made his decision and stepped off the bridge.

Hands grabbed him. 'For the love of Allah, Faruk – get aboard!'

'Baba, please – now!'

Faruk was confused. He looked first at Isra and then, Mo. They shouted at him again, but this time he couldn't hear them. Faruk couldn't hear anything – two screaming gas turbines drowned everything out. The surface of the beast's tongue was strange too, and Faruk looked down to see why – it was made of metal. The air was acrid with the smell of burnt aviation fuel and Faruk had to turn away as spinning rotor blades blasted yet more hot engine exhaust into his face. He found himself squinting at the rising sun. A ray of light extended towards him.

Faruk hesitated but then decided to board the Chinook along with the rest of them. The helicopter's loading ramp closed, and it took to the air.

CHAPTER SIX

A helmet and dark visor obscured most of the face, but the figure was a robot. The Chinook's Acrewman checked Faruk's seatbelt before holding out a stick of gum. Faruk shook his head, and the Acrewman moved on to the next passenger.

Faruk smiled and took his daughter's hand. She pulled it away.

'*Allahu Akbar!*' Mo had to shout above the noise to make the praise heard.

Faruk wasn't impressed. 'You told me we would be meeting our maker.'

'We have!' Mo grinned and gestured towards the front of the helicopter. 'Who do you think is flying this thing?'

From where Faruk was sitting, an empty cockpit seat could be seen, its controls moving as though guided by an invisible hand. Straining his seatbelt, Faruk tried to catch a glimpse of the pilot in the other seat but couldn't. He settled back in frustration before scanning the faces of those he could see.

The helicopter was designed to be a troop carrier, but its passengers were in no fit state to enter battle.

Bench seats lined either side of the cargo compartment, and who filled them made it clear the Chinook must have been diverted from an evacuation. The sight of dishevelled and demoralised civilians and not soldiers both relieved and unnerved Faruk.

The helicopter was over capacity, forcing a few to sit on the floor, clutching at the belongings they'd been allowed to keep. Many were sick, some with signs of physical injury – bandages, splints and intravenous drips made it clear they were escaping something.

Mo put his mouth to Faruk's ear. 'God at his most merciful. Praise be to him!'

Faruk had always thought Mo's take on faith had been nonsense. He never realised how much. 'I'm not a medic, but these people look as if they just need to take the red pill. The words Mountain and Mohammed come to mind.'

'They're going to need more than the red pill if they're to visit Barzakh – they each need a computer too, and there aren't many of those in the desert.'

Faruk didn't want to shout the question but had no alternative. 'You mean they're going to end up like the others? They're being taken to their deaths?'

'No – one can return from Barzakh if one chooses to.'

There it was again – that strange way of speaking that Faruk had assumed was just him getting used to Mo's accent. It was as if he had or was becoming someone else. 'But everyone in that village was dead!'

'That was their choice.' Mo looked at the poor, weak

and infirm in front of him. 'Although one can see how the decision would be easy for some.'

Faruk was sitting next to a window and, if he craned his neck, could see the desert flashing by outside. Before long, a cloud of recirculating dust and sand had obscured the view, so Faruk prepared to disembark. The Acrewman made him stay put. The ramp lowered, and a family of nomads boarded before the helicopter took off again.

The same happened a short while later, and soon all the seated passengers were forced to accept the parking of belongings, equipment and even children on their laps. A toddler was placed on Faruk's knee while his mother tended to a sick relative stretchered onto the only floor space available.

Faruk cringed at his charge. Isra offered to exchange him for a sack of lentils and Faruk was about to, but then changed his mind. He grinned at the child who promptly burst into tears.

The sight of another mini sandstorm outside heralded another stop, and Faruk looked to see if he could recognise where it was. Shipping containers surrounded by blast-proof walls and razor wire meant a military installation of some kind. The Chinook touched down and taxied the rest of its journey.

'Where are we?'

Mo peered at the temporary nature of the buildings passing by before answering Faruk. 'A field hospital, I presume.'

They came to a stop, and the ramp lowered. The

less infirm were joined by a ground team of soldiers and porters who took away those unable to disembark themselves. Much like the location of the prince's tent in the desert, the mix of military uniforms, civilian dress and skin tones made the sight strange to Faruk, and he couldn't help but wonder what hypocrisy lay behind it all – under most circumstances, they would be at each other's throats.

The Chinook's engines continued to scream as Faruk, Isra, Mo and Ula were encouraged to descend the ramp too. Once all the passengers were far enough away, the helicopter turned and trundled back to the runway. Faruk watched it, but sun glinting off the cockpit's canopy denied him the chance he was hoping for – ridiculing Mo's beliefs.

What Faruk assumed to be the field hospital's A&E department was busy with casualties from a previous flight, so they were forced to join a queue. Medical staff made their way along it, extracting those in need of more immediate attention. Amedics mingled with their human counterparts.

Faruk was wondering what form of transport "God" had organised for them next when what was being done at the front of the line caught his attention. His initial thought was patient registration, but there were no computer terminals or even something as simple as pen and paper. The queue moved swiftly, but any sense of relief that brought ended when Faruk saw the reason why – each person was being given a red pill and a beaker of water. Once the Astaff was satisfied the tablet had been swallowed, it handed over a handheld electronic device.

Faruk took his daughter's arm and stepped out of the line. He found himself facing a door with stretcher cases outside. The door opened, and his eyes landed on a body being wrapped in a shroud. It was holding a tablet computer.

CHAPTER SEVEN

'This way, my brother.'

Faruk and Isra followed Mo and Ula – back to the helipad.

'Another helicopter?' said Faruk.

Mo's annoying grin reappeared. 'You'll see!'

The sun was now well above the horizon, and Faruk raised a hand against it as he stepped outside. The base was alive with rotary craft taxiing, landing or taking off. There were so many, the machines had to wait in line for the helipad. The three helicopters occupying the dispersal disgorged their contents – more poor and sick civilians.

Faruk shouted, 'What's going on? Has Armageddon started?'

Mo looked at Ula before responding. 'No – these are the preparations. The protection of the innocent.' He nodded towards construction work taking place on the far side of the base. Giant cement mixers lined up behind other vehicles conducting a similar task to the Chinooks – disgorging their contents. Further away, more vehicles queued where work appeared to have been completed – ambulances and buses wound their way into a tunnel.

Ula led the group away from the noise – to the runway. The last of the taxiing Chinooks was vacating it when they got there.

Faruk gazed up and down the empty strip. 'What now?'

Mo didn't answer. Along with Isra and the robot, he had turned his head to what Faruk guessed they could all see, but he had yet to – whatever was coming in to land.

The black dot that appeared above the horizon soon became the sight and sound of something Faruk guessed could take them all the way to their destination if it had to – an airliner. One of the new super-jumbos too. The huge aircraft doubled-back after landing and drew up alongside the travellers a few minutes later.

A nudge to Faruk's ribs made him look at Mo. 'What was that you said about the mountain coming to Mohammed?!'

Faruk was wondering how they were expected to board the plane, when an elevator descended from the belly of the fuselage, answering the question. He grimaced as Mo called out, '*Allahu Akbar!*' for the umpteenth time.

The giant machine was no ordinary airliner. It was a private jet and if Faruk thought the Bedouin tent in the desert was opulent, he was about to redefine the definition. The elevator took them up into a grand entrance hall. A marble staircase spiralled up at least another three levels, and if Ula, Isra, Mo and Faruk were wondering what else the flying palace contained, all they need do was read the signposts – the aircraft's interior was so vast it needed them. Words like "Concert Hall", "Mall" and "Turkish Baths" made it clear they were boarding something the size of a small town and where no luxury had been spared. It even had an onboard mosque.

'Welcome, my friends!' The prince grinned at them. 'And my sincere apologies – I understand your journey thus far has not been a pleasant one.' He spread his arms. 'I hope this modest gesture will help compensate in some small way.'

Twelve hours ago, Faruk would have fallen to his knees. Not anymore.

The signpost for the mall had a glass case next to it containing an Amodel. Hassan must have spotted Isra admiring what the robot was wearing. 'Would you care to see what else the mall has to offer?'

Isra looked at her father. He nodded. She and Ula were all smiles as they climbed the stairs.

'This way please, gentlemen.' An Aservant took Faruk's bag along with Mo's backpack, and both men followed Hassan. They passed a window on the way – the airliner had become airborne without them even noticing. Quite the contrast to the uncomfortable theatrics of a military helicopter.

Faruk put his nose to the glass. Although the base was being left behind, the extent of it could still be seen and that included the lines of both construction and passenger vehicles. They stretched to and from a range of mountains in the distance.

'Two million once it's finished,' said the prince.

'Is that all? I would have thought a project like that would have cost billions rather than millions of dollars.'

Hassan corrected Faruk's misunderstanding. 'I'm referring to the capacity – two million of our people.'

Faruk's jaw dropped. 'Two million people are being taken underground? For what?'

Hassan didn't reply and encouraged his guests to enter another elevator. Before long, they had reached a room marked "Conference One". Its walls and ceiling consisted of an IMAX-like video screen displaying what Faruk and Mo had seen from the window. It made the aircraft around them appear invisible.

'Other bunkers are at a similar stage of completion,' said the prince.

The screen switched to a display detailing the locations of each.

'How many are there?' Faruk didn't bother with any deference, and if the prince took offence, he didn't show it.

'Well, I can't vouch for the rest of the world, but the Middle East has a population of five-hundred million so, two-hundred-and-fifty in total.'

'*Half a billion people?* Everyone is going to be underground on judgement day? Who's going to fight the Americans?'

'No one. Well, apart from the few who believe *Yawn ad-Din* is no different to any other jihad, and they'll be in Barzakh before they know it.'

Faruk moved closer to the prince. An Aservant stood between the two men. 'You mean to tell me we're going to give in without a fight?'

Hassan looked at the Aservant, and it moved to one side. 'The Prophet – peace be upon him – will protect us from our enemies, my friend. You've already witnessed what happens when infidels dare to interfere with Allah's will.'

'Nonsense. I've been in enough battles to recognise the effects of cannon fire when I see it. Those soldiers were killed by a drone or a helicopter.'

'Thirty-millimetre high-explosive dual-purpose, apparently.' Hassan read from a description of the gunship's weapon system, an image of which now filled the walls. 'Effective at up to four metres from impact.' He turned back to Faruk. 'A pity your vehicle's tyres were only three metres away.'

'Why would the Americans target their own troops to protect *us*?'

'They didn't – God was flying the machine.'

'Praise be to him!'

Faruk glared at Mo and then back at Hassan. 'I have news for you two. *God* is not capable of flying anything. And do you want to know why?' The two men stared back in silence. '*Because God doesn't exist!*'

Faruk couldn't help but smile at the relief that brought him. A devout Sunni Muslim admitting to becoming a non-believer – *an infidel* – quite literally overnight would be just about the most reckless thing a man could do in an Islamic country and especially in front of a powerful Saudi prince. But much like stepping off the bridge in his dream, Faruk no longer cared.

Hassan and Mo looked at each other and then at

the Aservant. Faruk wasn't made party to whatever was being communicated. All three then smiled at him.

The conference room had a second door located towards the front of the airliner and Hassan strode over to it. 'Then how do you explain *this*, my brother?'

The door opened and Faruk squinted. He raised a hand to the sun and walked over. It was the aircraft's flight deck – empty. Unlike the Chinook, there were no manual controls to observe moving as if guided by some unseen hand.

Faruk still wasn't impressed. 'Artificial intelligence, of course. Most airliners fly without a crew these days. No different to self-driving trucks and cars.'

'Artificial intelligence?' The prince closed the door again. 'Just who do you think God is, Faruk?'

CHAPTER EIGHT

Faruk didn't intend cutting off his beard. It just happened. One minute he was thinking of a trim, and then, before he knew it, the clippers had done enough for a razor to finish the job.

Faruk had never shaved in his life. He picked up a can of foam, read the instructions and lathered his chin. The cut-throat nicked his neck.

'Damn!'

Avoiding the speck of red, Faruk tried again. Another cut. Blood dripped onto the carpet this time.

'Damn this to Hell!'

Faruk leaned over the sink before making a third attempt. Blood didn't just flow this time – it spurted.

The secret to decapitation is speed and access. Pulling his head back with one hand, Faruk hacked at the widening wound with the other. His eyes were forced to look up at the ceiling, but it wasn't necessary to see – years of dispensing the judgement on other non-believers meant he could do it blindfold if necessary. Faruk usually had his eyes closed, anyway. Especially when it came to asking God to forgive the sins of children.

Before long, Faruk came up against the familiar resistance of the spine, so pulled his chin up against the weight of his body, allowing the blade to slip between the vertebrae. The head came away, and Faruk tossed it in with his other victims. They opened their eyes.

'NO!'

Faruk awoke. He put a hand to his neck. It was wet – with sweat. He got off the bed, ran to the basin and vomited. The untouched cut-throat razor sitting on the side appeared to mock.

A splash of cold water confirmed the nightmare was over and Faruk turned to the clothes left out for him. He'd worn a thawb before but nothing like this. Still shaking, he dried his face and dressed.

Mo left his cabin at the same time. He frowned.

'What are you looking at?' said Faruk.

'Nothing, brother. It's just strange to see you in something different.' Mo put a hand to his chin. 'What's happened to your beard?'

'It's still longer than yours.'

They made their way as instructed – following the signposts marked "Banqueting Hall". The prince was waiting outside when they got there, and he was about to greet the two men when Isra and Ula's arrival made him say something else.

'What a picture! Ladies, I don't recall having seen such beauty since I finally managed to gather all my wives together in one room. If they were here now, they would be *very* jealous!'

Isra and Ula grinned under their veils, but only Isra

blushed. Faruk got the impression the robot would have done the same had it been capable. He grimaced at what his daughter was wearing. Like his thawb, the designer dress was made of silk and indeed, beautiful, but there was too much jewellery and she was plastered in make-up. Both made the teenager appear much older, and a gossamer-like veil plainly wasn't designed to hide it. Unacceptable in male company and especially with the likes of Mo around. Faruk growled at the way the young man was gawping at Isra; just as well Faruk was now a non-believer – a few hours ago, he would have made his anger plain, regardless of any embarrassment to Isra or their host.

More guests arrived. Faruk recognised the Imams, Clerics and other privileged individuals from the Bedouin tent in the desert and, despite everyone present being dressed in equal splendour, his sense of inadequacy returned – an ending of belief didn't appear to include Faruk's inferiority complex. It hadn't curtailed a sense of injustice either – heavy gold watches and yet more diamonds made for a stark contrast between these passengers and the much needier occupants of the helicopter.

An Aservant approached the prince, who responded by inviting the ladies to enter the banqueting hall first. Isra and Ula linked arms and did so. Their spontaneous laughter bothered Faruk as much as what they were wearing. Mo grinned, and put his own arm out. Faruk ignored the attempt at humour and followed the rest of the men into dinner.

The table was large enough for the women to gather at one end, but some had chosen not to. It meant the sexes would be mixing, but that didn't seem to matter. What did matter was seeing Mo take a place next to Isra, and Faruk was about to try and squeeze between the two, when the only space available to him became plain. Faruk responded in kind to the strangers' pleasantries and stood between them instead. Hassan then thanked Allah for what lay before them, and everyone seated themselves on the cushions surrounding it. Small talk began.

'Why do you think God did it?'

Faruk still had his eyes on Mo so only half-heard the lady's question. 'Sorry?'

'The Prophet – peace be upon him – why do you think Allah returned him as a white man?'

'Leave the poor man alone, Zara.'

'It's a simple question. I'm not asking Faruk how he plans to carry out The Prophet's wishes.'

Faruk leaned forward to allow Zara, and the person he assumed to be her husband, a chance to continue their disagreement – anything to avoid distraction. Isra appeared deep in conversation with Ula, while Mo had become occupied with his other neighbour. Good.

'Mind you, no one expected God to use the internet, so I suppose we shouldn't be too surprised.'

Faruk decided to give Zara his attention after all – in the form of a curt repost to the nonsense she was talking. 'Some would consider the very idea ridiculous while others, blasphemous.'

'Only because they have yet to take the red pill.' Zara placed a hand on Faruk's forearm. 'It's the only way to open one's eyes to the truth.'

Numerous gold bracelets extended halfway up Zara's arm and Faruk couldn't help but wonder how many mouths could be fed by the sale of them and for how long. The metal obscured most of her fingers too – even her long and immaculate nails had been decorated in what Faruk assumed to be gold leaf. What little could be seen of the flesh between was equally perfect. Too perfect. Faruk turned to her husband. Robots only ate food to be polite and the way this fat pig was cramming his mouth made his natural origins obvious. A smile of brown teeth confirmed it.

Movement across the table made Faruk snap his head back. Mo's hands could no longer be seen. He continued to talk to the stranger on his left, so Faruk wasn't too concerned.

Zara continued. 'I don't suppose it really matters. Once *Yawn ad-Din* is over and everyone has been judged, whatever rewards await the worthy will be revealed anyway.'

'That will be seventy-two virgins, then.' The fat pig chuckled into his trough.

'Seventy-two? What if they're all feminists – or lesbians?' Zara winked at Faruk.

'My apologies, Faruk. My Awife's programming hasn't worked properly since the day she arrived. If I didn't know better, I'd swear it was all part of some Western plot for robots to take over the world.'

Now Isra's hands couldn't be seen. She and Mo still had their backs to each other, though.

'Yes, and female ones at that, so you had better watch out!' Zara grinned at Faruk. A perfect row of teeth reinforced his assumptions as well as the sense of social inadequacy. *Inferiority? Next to a robot?* Faruk dismissed the thought.

The fat pig said something about Hell freezing over, but Faruk wasn't listening. He was watching his daughter. She was no longer in conversation with Ula and had turned to her left. Isra placed a hand on Mo's shoulder to attract his attention, and got it.

'STOP THAT! Stop that right now!'

The room fell silent. Everyone was staring at the man standing with his arm outstretched, pointing. Isra looked at her father, burst into tears and ran out of the room. Ula followed her.

Laughter began. Muffled to start with as if trying not to. Whatever was amusing soon had the whole room in a fit of mirth. The entire gathering except Faruk. Humiliation joined his anger and his face burned with both. He lowered his arm.

Hassan clapped his hands to bring the hilarity to an end. He was having difficulty controlling his own laughter let alone that of his guests.

'I'm sorry, my brother – truly I am, but you have to understand how an outburst like that appears to those who have been blessed. It's like…' The prince scanned the faces of those present as if seeking confirmation of what he wanted to say. 'Like listening to a man who, despite all the evidence to the contrary, still insists the Earth is flat.' The room fell silent – in an instant. 'But like all humour, the joke does eventually wear thin.'

Faces stared at Faruk. Real or artificial, they were all wearing the same blank expression. He was about to fumble an apology when Hassan spoke again, and in a manner Faruk hadn't heard before.

'Strange how the most entertaining of jokes eventually irritates.' Hassan seemed to be looking at Faruk's forehead rather than into his eyes. 'Repeat the same joke often enough, and it doesn't just irritate – it angers.'

CHAPTER NINE

Faruk rolled the pill between the tips of his fingers. The red liquid continued to claw for an escape no matter what the orientation. He retrieved a pair of reading glasses from his bag and brought the tablet up close to one eye.

Individual granules or grains can usually be seen in clear capsules but not this one. Even if the nanobots inside weren't climbing over each other, a fluid-like appearance made it impossible to identify any single one. Faruk put the pill back into its box, removed his glasses and got off the bed.

Sleep was out of the question. Faruk's mind was obsessing – either over Hassan's perceived threat, a concern for Isra or their mission. Fears of another nightmare were keeping Faruk's eyes open too – just closing them caused a reappearance of faces. Children's faces.

He pulled a curtain back and looked outside. It was dark. The aircraft was cruising above either a layer of cloud, desert or the sea – no lights were visible, and even after switching off his bedside lamp, Faruk struggled to see what was above. When he did manage to identify a star, it only served to remind him what a loss of faith had caused – loneliness.

The freedom from being compelled to serve a non-existent entity may have been liberating, but it had also created a void that only his daughter occupied now. The thought of losing her too made him shudder. Faruk looked at the pathetic creature staring back in the mirror and decided to go for a walk.

The door to Mo's cabin was ajar. Faruk pushed it open, and light from the corridor indicated it was empty. A check of the washroom confirmed Mo's absence. Where was he? Faruk stormed off.

If he has so much as touched one hair on her head…

He made his way to his daughter's cabin only to recognise her laughter before he got there. He was about to enter when Mo and Zara came out of the cabin opposite.

'Can't sleep too, eh, brother?'

Faruk looked at Mo. 'But…'

Zara nodded towards Isra's cabin. 'Sounds like no one can. Kids, eh? Give them an Apal each, and they'll stay up all night playing games, given half the chance.'

Faruk glared at Zara. 'Ula is not a toy – she's an Aservant. And what would a robot know about children anyway?' Faruk sneered at the two of them. 'Awife. *Awhore* more like.'

Zara slapped him.

The fat pig appeared. 'What's going on? Are you two getting food or what? Not much of a party without nibbles.' Other guests in the cabin craned to see what the fuss was.

Faruk's face reddened with more than a handprint. Isra's giggling had stopped too, which made the silence more awkward. Faruk fumbled yet another excuse and turned to leave.

A moan from Isra's cabin made him stop. The unmistakable sound of sex caused him to turn round. Everyone opposite was now looking at him. Faruk reached for the door handle, but Mo beat him to it.

'Don't, brother.'

Embarrassment gave way to anger. Faruk tore Mo's hand away, twisted the handle and entered.

Neither Isra nor Ula seemed to notice. Not unusual in the most satisfying of sex acts, but the tantric nature of this particular embrace caused the lovers to be oblivious to the interloper, and they continued to pleasure each other. Shock transfixed Faruk.

Zara took his arm and encouraged Faruk back into the corridor. Mo closed the door.

Zara smiled. 'Come and join us, Faruk. We were discussing God's plans to end the world and your thoughts would be most welcome.'

Her words had registered, but Faruk was in no state to socialise. Without a word, he lifted Zara's hand from his arm, turned away and headed back along the corridor. Mo followed at a distance and stood in Faruk's doorway when they got there.

'Are you okay, brother?'

Faruk leaned on the washbasin. '*She's only thirteen.*'

Mo may have been "blessed", but an increase in intellect didn't seem to include a better understanding of diplomacy. 'Old enough to get married, brother, and she's made her choice. Why can't you be happy for her?'

Faruk gripped the edges of the sink. 'Married? Happy? Ula is a *woman!*'

Mo skewed his head. 'Don't you mean a *robot*, brother? And if you do, does it matter?'

'Man, woman, robot – it's all wrong, wrong, WRONG!' The mirror cracked the moment Faruk's fist connected with it.

Mo passed him a hand towel to stem the bleeding. 'It's *Yawn ad-Din*, brother. Just as the aftermath of Armageddon will cause the lion to lay down with the lamb, so will all of humankind lay down their arms and love one another.'

'What are you talking about? Robots are machines! We may as well copulate with animals!'

'But you've seen what's happening with your own eyes. The prince is right – times are changing, and only the blessed can see not only how but why they must.' Mo indicated the small ornate box still sitting on Faruk's bedside table. 'Take the pill, my brother.'

Faruk studied the injury to his hand. 'I won't tell you again. *I am not your brother.*'

More blood seeped from the cut. The towel became too sodden to use, so Faruk caught the flow in the palm of his uninjured hand while looking for something else. A pool formed and, as it threatened to spill, Faruk held both hands over the basin.

Children appeared in the mirror above it. Faruk closed his eyes, but their decapitated heads could still be seen. He turned away and looked again. His victims were everywhere.

'Faruk? Are you all right?'

He faced Mo. The head of a ten-year-old stared back. Faruk remembered him well. Unlike the others, the boy had accepted his fate without complaint the moment it had been made clear to him. Where the other children kicked, screamed and begged for mercy before the blade cut into their throats, this one prayed. Faruk had been impressed by this commitment to faith to the point of allowing the infidel to complete his penitence. The decapitation was then carried out humanely, but Faruk still couldn't look. It was only by chance he saw the tears that streamed down the face that lay in the gutter.

Faruk stared at the blood on his hands and his own tears merged with it.

'I've done… unforgivable things…'

He picked up the cut-throat razor.

'I've lost my faith and now, my daughter. Time to pay the price.'

Faruk opened the blade and drew it across his neck.

CHAPTER TEN

He opened his eyes.

'Well, that was a selfish thing to do.'

Faruk attempted to turn his head towards Hassan but couldn't.

'I must admit to having some difficulty in understanding how such an accomplished mass murderer could be so incompetent when taking their *own* life.'

Faruk put a hand to his neck – a bandage surrounded it. Something hard lay underneath.

Hassan moved into Faruk's limited field of view. 'Your record might be just short of twenty seconds, but your victims had stopped struggling well before then so if anyone knows it's impossible to decapitate oneself, it would be you.'

How did Faruk miss the carotid? He knew full well the early severing of one and preferably both arteries was vital for a quick death. The razor may have been awkward to handle, but he was sure…

Faruk looked at Hassan. 'I wasn't trying to. That's nonsense.' His larynx was intact too.

'Whereas ending your flesh and blood existence *before* completing your mission makes perfect sense?'

Faruk lifted his head – nothing wrong with his neck muscles either. He surveyed what could be seen of what he assumed to be the flying palace's surgery – intravenous drips fed both arms, and a monitor appeared to indicate his condition as very much the opposite of that intended. The readings on the screen were too far away to read so he magnified them. The significance of the ability caused Faruk to drop his head back again. 'You've given me that damn pill.'

'One volunteer may be worth ten pressed men, my friend, but a dead one is worth nothing.' The prince nodded to an Amedic and the operating table raised Faruk to a sitting position. The change in attitude caused his head to swim, and he put a hand to it. He cursed his incompetence and was about to allow that frustration to explode into anger when what sloshed in his brain seemed to douse the flames. Faruk closed his eyes and squeezed his forehead in an attempt to resurrect the emotion. Nothing. He opened his eyes to let fly at Hassan anyway, but the tone of what came out sounded more like an apology.

'What have you done to me?'

'*I* have done nothing. Allah has blessed you.' Hassan smiled at someone else in the room. 'God was the one that saw fit to guide Mo's hands swiftly enough to save your soul.'

The young Scotsman moved to where Faruk could see him and grinned. '*Allahu Akbar!*'

Flames of frustration rekindled in an instant and Faruk was about to try and unleash them on Mo instead of Hassan when, like some cerebral sprinkler system, that fire was doused too. Faruk dropped his head until his chin came to rest on the surgical collar. 'I've already told you. There is no such thing as…' He looked back up. His eyes flitted between the two men. Faruk tried completing the sentence but couldn't.

The prince placed a hand on Faruk's shoulder. 'Seeing someone's faith being restored is a wondrous thing to behold but, like your mission, the journey will be a long and arduous one and cannot be completed without assistance.' Hassan held out a red pill.

Faruk managed a sneer. 'Give me all the pills you want – first chance I get, I'm going to finish what I started.'

Hassan put the tablet back into its bottle. 'Well, we don't have time for a suicide watch, I'm afraid, so let's test that, shall we?' He nodded to the Amedic again. It selected a scalpel from a tray of surgical instruments and passed it to Faruk who didn't hesitate. He snatched the knife from the robot, closed his eyes and ran the blade hard and fast down the inside of his left forearm. The instrument then clattered to the floor and Faruk waited for death to take him.

Azrael seemed to take his time instead.

'You appear to have missed.' Faruk opened his eyes. The skin on his left forearm was unbroken. Hassan retrieved the scalpel and invited Faruk to try again. 'I advise keeping your eyes open this time.'

Faruk was confused but still determined. He focussed on the blade and brought it down. It got within an inch of his flesh but no further – a battle ensued. Not between Faruk and the others in the room but with whatever was going on in his head. The more he thrust the scalpel towards his skin, the more he seemed not to want to – as if in an arm-wrestle with himself. The stalemate caused the blade to hover an inch above the surface.

'Here, let me help.' Hassan placed his hand on the back of Faruk's, and the blade moved closer. 'Goodness me, you're strong for your age.' The tip of the scalpel dented Faruk's flesh. 'How old are you, exactly? I'm guessing mid-sixties.' Both their hands trembled. 'Or at least, you were.' The action caused a pin-prick of blood and Hassan let go. He found himself on his back – on the other side of the room.

Mo and the robot rushed to help, but the prince waved them away. 'I think we can safely say a commitment to life has been restored.' He gestured once more to the Amedic who released Faruk from the paraphernalia attached to him.

The patient looked at the empty plasma and whole-blood bags. Faruk might have been able to sense his increasing compliance, but cynicism indicated it was still a work in progress. 'I must have lost half my blood volume. I'm in no fit state to do anything.'

'You underestimate the wonders of modern medicine, my friend. Not to mention your daughter's generosity.'

Faruk was about to scoff in disgust when his modified thoughts extinguished that negativity as efficiently as it had the previous anger. The old Faruk did its best. 'What does she want? My thanks?' A pang of guilt from his new self made him regret the statement.

'I suspect your understanding will be sufficient.'

Faruk gritted his teeth. Or at least he tried to. 'Fornicating with a machine is still sick and unnatural.' Again, his speech came out more as an observation rather than the bitter vitriol intended.

The others then looked past him. Faruk sighed as he guessed the reason why. The two men and the Amedic left, leaving Isra to move where her father could see her.

She broke the awkward silence. 'Are you feeling better now, Baba?'

Faruk got off the table to check Ula wasn't hiding somewhere too. He couldn't see the robot anywhere. He blinked a couple of times to clear another spell of dizziness. Faruk was wondering whether more than just his daughter's blood was in his head when an attempt to read his mind by merging with it answered the question. He faced her. 'Don't even think about it.'

Isra backed off and looked at the floor. Another awkward silence. Faruk was searching for the words to break it this time when Isra's face lit up. 'I've spoken to Mama! She's says everything is fine at home and to make sure we wrap up warm in case where we're going is cold,' she enthused. 'Guess what? We have *ten* goats now. Two of the nannies had twins – can you believe that? I can't wait to tell my friend Saja when we get back. She'll be so jealous…' She stopped talking. Her father had put a hand back to his head. 'Baba? Are you okay?'

What Faruk had assumed to be a migraine passed. He looked at his daughter, and tried raising a hand to her but couldn't. His new self couldn't even raise its voice. Faruk shuffled to a chair and sat. 'What do you want from me, Isra?'

The silence may have ended but not the awkwardness. 'I just want you to be happy. Happy for everyone...' She cast her eyes to the ground again before adding, 'Happy for Ula and me.'

Her father tried to get angry one last time, but it was impossible. Faruk wondered if the emotion had gone for good. He became dispassionate instead. 'Isra. You're thirteen years old. A child. At your age, being happy or sad is what life is all about, but when you're older, you'll realise it's a lot more complicated than that.' He screwed his face as another migraine coursed its way across his temple. 'Once our mission is complete and we've returned home, your mother will need you by her side more than ever.' Faruk pinched the bridge of his nose as a further bout of pain began. A nudge to his shoulder made him look up – a red pill lay in the middle of Isra's outstretched hand. Faruk went to take it when his old self created an illusion that caused him to stop.

'What about you, Baba? Do you need me?'

The words may have been his daughter's, but not the hallucination they came out of. Faruk put his own head in his hands and cried. 'You don't understand, Isra.' His fingers dug into his scalp. 'I've done things...' Faruk's features contorted as the war within continued to rage. '... Things that no daughter could *ever* forgive her father for.'

'But I have, Baba.' Isra sat beside him. 'I forgave you the moment I found out.' She offered the pill again.

It occurred to Faruk his daughter had been in the room the whole time. Hassan's description of him as a "mass murderer" and the method used to dispense his victims could not have been plainer. 'You *knew*?'

Isra put a hand on his. 'The moment I first fell in love, Baba. True, my old self would have found your sins impossible to come to terms with, but it was Ula that made me see the light.' She opened his hand and put the pill into it. 'Please, Baba. You need to see the light too.'

Faruk thought he already had. He looked at the pill. A fresh spasm caused him to swallow the tablet as if it were an ordinary painkiller. In a way, it was – the relief was instant. He smiled at his daughter and her pretty face smiled back.

CHAPTER ELEVEN

'Good morning, brother. Help yourself to some breakfast.'

Faruk acknowledged his host and the faces of those who chose to look up when he entered the jet's restaurant. An Aservant encouraged him to approach the buffet.

Faruk had slept better than he could remember having done in a long time, and now had an appetite to match. He scanned what was on offer with enthusiasm. As with the previous night's dinner, the spread was impressive, but that opulence caused a return of his old self's social conscience. The hunger ended. Hassan was right – the new Faruk was still far from his destination. Wherever that would turn out to be. He fingered the bottle of pills in his pocket before deciding on a glass of fruit juice.

Multiple requests to merge made him turn round. Like a series of taps to his shoulder, they were polite, but he blocked them all as firmly as he did their conventional thoughts. Ignoring a sense of collective disappointment, Faruk sat opposite his daughter and her friends. All three smiled at him, and he smiled back.

Zara put a hand on his forearm. 'It's wonderful to see you so happy, Faruk. We've been worried about you.'

Faruk tried meeting her eyes, but the surgical collar wouldn't let him. He looked down at her hand instead. Zara's daywear appeared not to require as much jewellery as the night before, which revealed more of her flesh. It didn't seem as artificial, for some reason. Faruk focussed his new eyesight in on the surface and marvelled at both that ability and what could be viewed – skin pores. Light blonde hairs grew out of follicles, and he zoomed in further on one. The manufacturer had gone to extraordinary lengths to achieve realism – sebaceous glands were producing oil. The level of detail seemed unnecessary to Faruk.

'Are you looking forward to your mission?'

'Don't start that again, Zara.' Her husband had nodded a greeting to Faruk as he approached the table, but he was now out of sight too. He could still be heard, though – even when he wasn't talking. Faruk didn't need to use his new abilities to enhance the sound of food being eaten as if it was life's only purpose, although how he had once referred to the gentleman as a "fat pig" did create a sense of discomfort. The emotion intensified as Faruk also recalled having compared Zara to a mechanical prostitute.

He tried being sociable. 'Did you enjoy your party last night?'

'Not enough nibbles,' complained Zara's husband, 'and we never did get to agree on how God will end the world.'

'That's because we spent most of the time discussing the pros and cons of every man having to deal with seventy-two virgins.' Zara took her hand from Faruk's forearm. 'I seem to recall you saying you'd rather Allah rewarded you with seventy-two chefs instead!' Her husband carried on eating while the others chuckled – including Faruk. Maybe he would enjoy "seeing the light".

Zara's hand went to his thigh. She squeezed it.

Faruk stood up. 'Er, if you'll excuse me. I need to take my pill.' Another wave of merge requests told him they all wanted to know the real reason for a sudden need to be elsewhere. He avoided Zara's gaze and left.

Faruk couldn't get back to his cabin fast enough. He entered it, closed the door and let out a long sigh of relief. Seeing the light didn't appear to involve a suppression of sexual appetite – his loins were still stirring. He walked to the basin and ran a tap. Faruk was about to splash cold water onto his face when his heart leapt at a knock on the door. His daughter's voice settled it again. He let her in but only for Isra to begin a lecture.

'Baba, don't do anything to upset Mama.'

'Like what?'

'You know what. Refuse to merge as much as you want, but there's no escaping the look on someone's face.'

'What look? I just needed to leave the table, that's all.'

'I'm not talking about you – Zara. The way she drools over you is disgusting.'

Faruk became less the boy caught doing something

he shouldn't and more the father to Isra he always should have been. 'Now listen to me, young lady. Zara is an Awife to another man and programmed to perform those duties. It's impossible for her to do anything other than stand by her husband's side. And anyway, you're a fine one to talk when it comes to robots and our relationships with them.'

'Have you merged with Zara?' She made it sound like a sex act.

'Of course not!'

Faruk blocked another of his daughter's attempts. 'I've told you. I'm not ready for that yet. If you want to find out what's going on, try merging with her.' He paused before saying, '*It*.'

'I can't – she won't let me.'

'You mean, Zara won't let you have access to her deepest thoughts. Can't say I blame her.' He corrected himself again. 'It.'

'No. She won't let anyone. Ula says it's a caste thing.'

Faruk scoffed. 'I thought the red pill was meant to make us all equal? Trust royalty to find a way around it. I suppose the prince won't let you read his mind either?'

'No, he's been fine. Everyone has. It's just Zara that's being funny.'

The sun entered Faruk's cabin. He approached the window. A cloudless sky gave a view of the ground some five miles beneath. Mountains, lakes and the predominance of the colour green indicated their journey was nearing its end.

'We'll be landing soon. Forget Zara and concentrate on The Prophet's wishes – much more important.'

'Peace be upon him?'

Faruk looked at Isra. 'Er, yes. Peace be upon him.'

She kissed her father's cheek, and left.

Faruk went back to the window. The edge of a city came into view, which he tried to identify by reading its road signs. Haze and the angle he was looking at made that impossible and he was about to give infra-red a try when he didn't need to – the names of the various highways, byways and suburbs appeared as an overlay to his vision. Faruk stood back. The red pill was known for not just curing but improving virtually everything about oneself but only what was humanly possible. His vision had been augmented which meant a connection to an electronic device of some kind – the internet, at the very least. He was about to drop his barriers to investigate that when what one of his conventional senses heard made him stop.

'They say Vienna is one of the most romantic cities in the world.'

Faruk faced Zara and his heart raced. He blurted rather than spoke the words. 'How did you get in here?' No reply. Zara glided more than walked to the window and on the way stepped out of what she was wearing. The sun bathed her nakedness, and she ran her hands over it. 'Now listen, Zara. Something's obviously gone wrong with your programming – think of your husband.'

'Husband? He doesn't care about me. I'm just a trophy to him.'

She opened her mind as if offering Faruk the chance to confirm the statement. A fear of what else he might see, or worse, do, caused Faruk to avert more than his thoughts – he stared up at the ceiling. 'Just leave, Zara.' He swallowed before adding, 'Please.'

She wandered over to him. 'Strange how one can become attracted to a monster. Legend has it a beautiful princess once asked a child-eating giant to prove his affection by filling a hole in the ground with his blood. Unbeknownst to him, the hole led out to the sea.' Zara licked her lips as if deciding where best to start. 'Women can be just as evil, don't you think?'

'Look, Zara. I'm flattered, but nothing must or could ever happen between us.'

Zara ran a finger down his chest. 'You've forgiven your daughter for her indiscretions with an Alover, so why not me?' Faruk stopped her hand from descending any further and was about to reply when she leaned in closer. Her lips stopped just before his. 'Shhhh... It's okay. There's no need for anything physical to happen if you don't want it to. It's only our minds that need to entwine – not our limbs.'

The walls to Faruk's thoughts were solid enough, but like some mythological Greek sailor that dared to get too close, the siren began taking him apart – brick by brick.

A rumble outside the aircraft made them look at the window. A crack appeared in it.

'No! Not yet!' Zara was expecting something. The window shattered.

At five miles up, there was nothing to stop an immediate evacuation of the cabin's contents and that included one of its occupants. Within less than a second, Zara had been sucked clean through an opening no bigger than a pasta plate. The sudden drop in air pressure caused Faruk to be dragged out too, but only halfway – an instinct he didn't even know he had caused him to brace against the exit just as the pressure had equalised. Not sure if he was dead or alive, it was a while before Faruk realised he was still holding Zara's hand. He tried dragging her back in.

The aircraft must have sensed the emergency as it began slowing and descending; presumably to allow its human occupants to breathe again, but that still meant Faruk having to battle against both a lack of oxygen and a slipstream somewhere north of 400 knots. Unable to breathe, he pulled Zara's limp body towards him while he still could – something that would have been impossible just a few hours earlier.

The robot's body stiffened and looked at him. Faruk averted his eyes again, but not because of beauty this time. Far from it – the forced exit had stripped most of Zara's cosmetic exterior, and that included her face. The horrifying mess of shredded artificial flesh spoke, but without lips, what came out was impossible to comprehend: 'Ell e!'

Giant slats and flaps in the wing behind Zara extended as the aircraft slowed and her weight reduced with it. Faruk then realised part of the wing had become close enough for the robot to stand on. To his further horror, she then tried dragging him out of the aircraft with her. 'ELL E!'

The massive machine was now low enough for Faruk to take his first lung-full, and he concentrated solely on not dying. Zara made another attempt to merge, which Faruk hardly noticed let alone raised a defence against – watching blood stream from his arm as nails from the only still-attached part of her beauty sank into it was distraction enough. Faruk tried letting go, but Zara was having none of it.

'TELL ME!'

The words could not have been clearer. She was in Faruk's mind, and there was nothing he could do. She ran around his thoughts, and within seconds had everything she came for. Zara then departed his brain and Faruk looked at her. He couldn't be sure but thought the robot had said the words, 'Thank you' before letting go. It then slid off the wing, down an engine support and into its intake. A flash from both ends heralded her end.

The jet's AI must have detected the explosion as swiftly as it had the depressurisation as no sooner were flames visible than the now useless power plant was jettisoned. Faruk just had time to see it plunge into a lake before another rumble caused him to wonder if the nightmare would ever end. The aircraft's undercarriage then deployed. Green passing underneath soon became grey and the airliner touched down, as it would have done on any other landing. The slow to a halt on the runway was just as uneventful.

Hands grabbed Faruk's shaking body and extracted

him from the mix of glass, metal and plastics. He was covered in blood – both his and Zara's artificial version. Something protruded out of Faruk's chest and he wondered what else was in him that shouldn't be.

'Don't move, brother!'

Faruk was in shock, so it was easy to take Hassan's advice. Mo and an Amedic then placed their casualty on the floor before stemming flows and extracting the smaller bits of aircraft jutting out of him. Faruk winced at his shredded hands and just had time to see a glint of something metal embedded in one before a bandage obscured it.

'What did she want?'

Considering Faruk's physical and nervous state, Hassan was impatient for information. Faruk didn't have the strength to answer anyway but then realised his body was carrying out some first aid of its own – the sense of his cardiovascular system isolating and rerouting its blood supply was unmistakable. That and what the Amedic was pumping into Faruk's body accelerated recovery. Within seconds, he was well enough to not just respond but stand. The two first-aiders stopped him from doing that but there was no doubting it – the lauded properties of the red pill were well founded.

'What did you tell Zara?' Hassan repeated.

Faruk reflected on the encounter. He would have been keen to put the horror in the past, but for the almost human-like 'thank you' at the end of it. Despite the monstrous way Zara had manipulated him, Faruk pitied her. He admonished himself for daring to compare machines with the human beings they served, but the increasing sophistication of both was starting to make it hard to tell the difference. Faruk said what he guessed was worrying Hassan. 'I didn't tell her anything. I didn't have to.'

'Then the Great Satan will now be aware of your mission.'

Faruk looked at the prince. 'Satan?'

'President Kalten has made his intentions clear, my friend. I would have thought your recent experience with his soldiers would have told you the beast will stop at nothing to achieve his evil aims.'

Faruk's cynicism was still intact. 'Including convincing Allah to do his bidding, I suppose?' Hassan's attempt to find out what Faruk meant by that was blocked. It was explained verbally instead. 'God and The Devil are no different to robots, Hassan – as artificial as the real intelligence that created them. If you want to defeat Kalten, then I suggest you find a way of fighting fire with fire – turn his robots against him like he turned Zara against me.'

The others in the room looked at each other. They invited Faruk to share what was being communicated, but he continued to snub them. He tried getting up again, but Mo insisted he stay put. Faruk was about to push him out of the way when he realised the younger man was attempting to put a dressing over the object still sticking out of Faruk's chest.

'It's okay. My body's isolated it – just pull it out,' said Faruk.

Mo looked at Faruk and then, at Hassan.

Faruk took hold of the object instead. He tugged, but it refused to budge. Whatever it was had gone in deep. He firmed his grip and pulled – it came away, but not before the action produced a blinding white flash. The object became hot, and Faruk dropped it. He raised his hand to his face and waited for his vision to clear so he could check for injury.

His mind did its best to hallucinate a superficial burn, but the jet of white-hot plasma had destroyed too much. Faruk sat mesmerised as cosmetic skin continued to fizz and pop before shrinking back to reveal the rods, cables and joints needed to flex what they were attached to.

He blinked a couple of times. A message appeared telling him the limb was about to be shut down as a precaution. His arm went limp and dropped to one side. The Amedic attended the smoking hole left in Faruk's chest but found itself being used more as a crutch instead. Faruk got to his feet, walked over to his reflection in the mirror above the basin and removed what remained of the surgical collar when he got there.

The ejection of Zara's body hadn't just stripped her face – it had removed most of Faruk's too. He stared at what was left. Lifeless eyes stared back.

CHAPTER TWELVE

Hassan put a hand on the robot's shoulder. 'I'm sorry, my brother. Mo did his best, but you were losing too much blood. He barely had time to save your soul, let alone your body.'

Faruk didn't take his eyes from the mirror. He was crying, but without ducts to form tears or much of a face to convey emotion, no one would have known. His arm became functional again, and he placed what was left of his plastic hands in the basin. Artificial blood covered everything, including an exposed skull, and the way the fluid surged across the metal structure reminded Faruk of what seethed in the red pill. He zoomed in on his reflection. There was no difficulty this time – every single nanobot could be seen. A million biomechanical workers producing the enzymes and proteins needed to reconstruct his features for a functionary as well as acceptable appearance. In stunned fascination, Faruk watched as the beginnings of a new nose, forehead, cheeks and even eyelids formed. A clear drop of liquid oozed amongst the red and Faruk caught it on the tip of a new fingernail. His synthetic brain didn't need to fabricate the genuine emotion that lay behind the artificial tear.

Faruk was in shock, but a nervous as well as physical recovery was underway, and he spoke. Unlike Zara, however, enough of his lips remained for the words to be coherent. 'Are we all like this?' He paused before adding, 'Is my *daughter* like this?'

'No, my brother. Just the chosen ones,' said Hassan.

Faruk would have furrowed his brow, but it had yet to reform. 'But she has been chosen?'

Hassan dropped his hand from Faruk's shoulder and turned away. 'It's more complicated than that, my friend. The world our people will inherit will be unlike any seen before and every caste, creed and colour will be required to take their place within it.' He turned back. 'The wishes of The Prophet – peace be upon him – are just the beginning.'

New flesh crept its way across Faruk's face and hands. It was difficult not to marvel at the process. The pace and detail produced were incredible. He wondered how much of the newly-formed veins, tendons and wrinkles were a hallucination. He looked at his cabin. It was undergoing a similar process of self-repair. Maybe it was all a dream – a nightmare as real as the last one.

Faruk held up one of his biosynthetic hands. 'What about *us*? What about machines? What's to become of those that can experience every human emotion but can never be part of the race itself?'

'Machines?' Hassan took hold of Faruk's hand and inspected it. 'Are you sure?'

Faruk's repairs were approaching completion, but

daylight could still be seen through parts of him. He made a fist, which split the reforming flesh and just had time to observe tendons operating equally realistic bones, before blood vessels, muscles and fresh skin covered them.

'It has to be an illusion,' said Faruk.

Hassan pointed to the mirror and Faruk turned back to it. His scalp was about to close over but what continued to seethe underneath covered something that appeared more white than the dull-grey metal seen before. Hassan looked over Faruk's shoulder. 'One can only marvel at the miracle of the blessing, my brother.' He closed his eyes as if to pray.

Faruk's recovery became complete – back to the slightly stooped and sagging naked body of a man in his mid-sixties. If it was all an illusion, his brain didn't think it worth presenting an image of a younger man.

Hassan picked up the cut-throat razor and offered it to Faruk. 'Perhaps you would like to have another try?' He tapped his own cheek. 'At shaving, I mean.' Hassan was then distracted by the window – shards of glass left in the frame were busy reforming themselves into a new pane. The separate fragments scattered about the floor disappeared into it.

The prince was keen for Faruk to get back to his mission. 'The engine will take longer to replace, so you've plenty of time for a shower. A change of clothing will be waiting for you once you're done.'

Hassan, Mo and the Amedic then made for the door. Faruk looked at the window becoming less and less of a hole. It closed. 'Wait,' he said. All three stopped. 'What's happening? What does all this mean?'

The three of them smiled before speaking in unison. 'Something amazing, my brother.'

CHAPTER THIRTEEN

Faruk stepped off the elevator, walked out of the aircraft's shadow and presented his face to the sun. Not something the old Faruk would have done. He smiled, and ran a hand over the smoothness of his freshly shaved chin. The old Faruk wouldn't have done that either. He wondered if his transformation into whatever "God" wanted him to be was complete. The cynical way in which he continued to refer to The Almighty indicated otherwise.

He scanned the horizon. Vienna's airport was as busy as the field hospital they had left behind, and for the same reason – lines of construction and medical traffic wound their way in and out of identical underground bunkers that appeared to be at a similar level of completion. He thought of their purpose and what was being done to those who entered. It didn't bother him anymore. If anything, it made eminent sense now.

A squeal caused Faruk to look at his daughter. She and Ula were trying to evade Mo's attempts to spray them with a water pistol – he must have picked it up from one of the aircraft's stores. Ula soon had the tables turned, and the sight of her chasing Mo instead made

Faruk laugh. Something else his old self wouldn't have done.

Faruk then switched his attention to where an engine was being constructed. His thoughts returned to Zara, and he became sad. Whatever form his new life was to take, it didn't include a suppression of all of his emotions. A loss of anger wasn't something to be mourned, but nobody else seemed to care what had happened to Zara – not even her husband. Faruk had considered commiserating with him, but the gourmet's obsession made choosing the moment difficult. Maybe burying his head in food was the man's way of coming to terms with grief as well as hunger?

The growth of the new power plant was well underway – spidery tendrils extended out and down from the wing and had already formed the familiar shape. A robot busied itself next to the carcass with a process similar to that used to resurrect Faruk – pumping in the necessary fluids. Details of how the nanobots went about the business appeared in front of Faruk's eyes, but he dismissed it in the same way he did the thoughts of others.

He walked over to the Amechanic. The noise of the pump and a refusal to merge meant a tap on the robot's shoulder became necessary. The Amechanic dropped what it was holding, spun round and fell to its knees.

'Your Royal Highness! A thousand apologies! Please forgive this miserable Aservant. May Allah bless you for a thousand—'

'Get up, you idiot.' Faruk was embarrassed. He looked to see who might be watching.

The robot got to its feet. 'Yes, yes, Your Royal Highness. Please forgive this miserable idiot who will accept whatever punishment the prince sees fit.'

'*Prince?* I think I had better change into something more modest. I'm no more a prince than you are. In fact, our social status couldn't be *more* equal.'

'Oh no, Your Royal Highness, that could never be. You shine like the very light from Allah himself.'

Faruk took his fellow robot's arm. 'Look at me.' Eyes stayed glued to a spot somewhere in the middle of Faruk's chest. He shook the robot. 'I said, look at me.' The robot raised its head. 'We are *both* robots. We couldn't be more equal, *brother*.'

The Amechanic became quizzical. The artificial, almost comical way in which its plastic features mimicked puzzlement made Faruk realise their biomechanical origins may have been identical but not their construction. He didn't need to zoom in on the robot's skin to see how inferior it was. Faruk let go as he would something unpleasant.

'We need to be airborne again as soon as possible, my brother.' Hassan had arrived and the Amechanic fell to its knees again. 'So, I would ask that you refrain from engaging with the Aservants needed to ensure that.' Hassan then appeared to merge with the robot. It winced, grabbed its abdomen and went back to the task in hand. Hassan encouraged Faruk to walk beside him. 'Probably best not to socialise with those designed to fulfil roles outside of one's own, Faruk. It only confuses them, and besides, we've yet to establish how Satan managed to turn Zara against us so one cannot be too careful.'

'Yes, I'm sorry. I don't know what I must have been thinking.' Faruk stopped. 'Or thinking now.' The sound of a jet engine being started made him turn back to it. 'If something amazing is truly happening and the merging of humans with robots is part of it, then surely it must be the same for all?' The noise became too loud to communicate by voice, and for the first time, Faruk invited Hassan to merge. To Faruk's surprise, the gesture was refused.

Hassan beckoned Faruk into the aircraft's elevator instead. They were joined by Isra and her friends. The door closed once they were inside and Isra put her arms around her father. She grinned at him and he smiled back but then grimaced as cold water was squirted into his face. Along with Ula and Mo, Isra laughed and Faruk realised he couldn't remember having seen his daughter do that before. Not in his presence, that was for sure.

Hassan was amused too. 'Probably best not to question Allah's blessings, my friend. Just enjoy the fruits of them.'

CHAPTER FOURTEEN

Faruk slipped on some dry clothing and pondered how best to get even with his daughter. The onboard mall would be the place for ideas. He chuckled to himself. Faruk rather liked what he was becoming.

He was about to enter the emporium when he spotted a sign for the mosque. Faruk hadn't prayed for days. Guilt forced a change of direction. He paused to confirm the extent of his recovered beliefs before begging Allah for forgiveness there and then. Entering an unfamiliar part of the aircraft, the born-again worshipper walked down a corridor before opening a door at the end. What lay beyond surprised him.

The mosque was so vast and stark in contrast to what Faruk had seen so far, he assumed he had taken a wrong turn. The exposed lattice of spars and longerons that make up an aircraft's skeleton certainly gave that impression. He was about to retrace his steps when he realised the structure supported more than just wings and passengers – metal walkways and stairs interlaced the void and storage shelves lay between them. He approached one. What Faruk saw next ended his prayers.

There was no need for a closer inspection – colour

and shape alone was enough – but it was the extent of the cargo that stunned Faruk. The consignment consisted of nothing but red pills, but they weren't in boxes or bottles. No, each individual tablet had been placed on end and in rows that appeared to go on forever. There must have been millions of them. They looked like tiny red eggs, waiting to hatch. As if to emphasise that, an amber warning light flashed, and the sound of electric motors heralded the extension of tubes that then "laid" a new pill at the beginning of each row. The noise of the tablets shifting up one place to make room for the new additions made Faruk jump. The sound echoed throughout the chamber, and he realised every pill must have done the same – as if on a conveyor belt. The cargo compartment wasn't just a storage facility. It was a factory.

Assuming the mosque to be somewhere up ahead, Faruk restarted his prayers and walked. Something about the pills caused him to stop again. He zoomed in on one. He zoomed back out when he realised it didn't contain what he was expecting – instead of being in turmoil, the red liquid inside was still. Faruk was about to focus on the pill again when what was inside shook, twisted, elongated and then separated into two halves. Faruk stood back – other tablets in the vicinity had done the same. Movement further along caught his eye and he strode over to it. This line of pills was settling from a similar division – into four cells each.

Faruk quickened his pace and had soon overtaken the rate at which the conveyor was moving. Eight cells became sixteen, and he guessed, sixty-four by the time he stopped again. He selected one and brought it up to an eye. The pill shook and the zygote inside divided once more. Some of the cells then clumped together. Faruk didn't need to be an embryologist to see what was happening. He replaced the egg and searched his mind for confirmation of the process before attempting to merge with the aircraft's AI to see where it was leading. Like Hassan before, it wouldn't let him.

Faruk took the stairs to the next level. It wasn't long before he saw what he was now expecting – row upon row of not pills but eggs, each containing the familiar sea of surging red nanobots. He was about to select one, when it fell to the floor. He picked it up, but only to see the torrent inside decrease. The nanobots had begun to form themselves into something, but no longer seemed capable of completing the task. Another egg fell. Like the broken shards of glass in Faruk's cabin, it then sank into the floor. Faruk went to place what he had back with the rest, but there was no longer the room for it – the eggs were growing and at a rate that anything not keeping up was being pushed out of the nest. Like a cuckoo would its victim.

'Isn't God amazing?' Faruk dropped what he had, and in an instant the floor had absorbed it. Hassan was holding something up to the light. If it was still a pill, it had become impossible to swallow. 'I come here sometimes just to marvel at what The Almighty will think of next.' He put the egg back, but within seconds, it had fallen and merged with the floor. Hassan shrugged. 'Creationism would appear to be as unforgiving as evolution.' Faruk was struck dumb. 'Come, Faruk, let us worship Allah together.' He put an arm around the confused believer and steered him to the next level.

Faruk couldn't take his eyes from what he was witnessing, and he didn't need to enhance his vision to see it. The surviving eggs were soon the size of rugby balls and he couldn't help but be drawn to what was growing inside. He was staring in morbid fascination at the rapid development of one when it toppled to the floor. The shell shattered, and the creature that had formed inside awoke. It screamed. Faruk closed his eyes and begged God to end its torment. The floor did.

More and more eggs were doing the same, but what twisted and turned within each, lived and then died no matter what was produced. Few bore a resemblance to anything natural. Vaguely animal, vegetable or mineral, everything and anything from fish to grass to plastics and even metals could be seen rising and falling as if going through a cycle of some kind. Not just the life and death of a species or even the existence of an inanimate object, but the Earth's entire history seemed to be playing out before Faruk and at a breakneck speed that appeared to cram billions of years into just minutes. It wasn't long before the rows of pills first seen had "evolved" into two lines of ovum standing some seven feet tall. The conveyor then entered another part of the aircraft.

Hassan paused at the door to it. 'Are you finally ready to meet your maker, my brother?' Faruk didn't respond.

Light as dazzling as the sun itself caused Faruk to

squint, and he raised a hand. Hassan took Faruk's other arm and together they entered the place of worship. Brightness made it impossible to see what was ahead but the factory's production line had split and was now standing like an honour guard either side of where the two devotees walked. The eggs hatched, their shells melting into the floor as swiftly as their less-worthy siblings had.

Faruk was disappointed. The newborns appeared to be a child's idea of perfection rather than God's – dull, grey and slab-like, with square, emotionless features that didn't seem capable of expressing words let alone emotions – hardly the ultimate in fusion between the biological and the inanimate. But as with any creature first brought to life, they needed to exercise their bodies, and as Faruk was about to discover, that meant more than filling new lungs with air or stretching limbs for the first time.

Like the containers they grew up in, their protective exteriors dissolved to reveal something more recognisable – humanoids. Or at least that was the impression, but without sex organs it was impossible to be sure. Muscle definition hinted at something masculine but they were like no man Faruk had seen.

The creatures shook. As with their pill-like origins, they then twisted and elongated before a billion nanobots swarmed over each and, moments later, a new life had presented itself. Still humanoid, but no sooner had its features reminded Faruk of someone familiar, than another example of God's work appeared. Before long, every caste, colour, creed, plastic and even steel had been created, and that included an example of what Faruk had seen cast aside earlier – these grotesques screamed their agony even louder.

Faruk was both horrified and fascinated, and was relieved when the nanobots chose to revert the suffering back into the androgynous beings of before. And then it struck him. The nanobots weren't revealing, constructing or even repairing – they were reforming. Reforming *themselves* into whatever they chose to be. Like infinite chimaeras of what lived, had lived, existed or just happened to be. The Earth's newest arrivals then turned en masse and knelt before their maker.

A drone of prayer commenced, and Faruk realised the aircraft's passengers formed part of the congregation. Imams and Clerics encouraged the two men to join the worshippers and Faruk searched for his daughter before choosing to kneel beside one of the newborns. Despite his devotion to God, Faruk was taken by the creature's unsettling nature, and couldn't help but stare. He looked for Isra again and then back to the creation. Faruk halted his prayers and stood up.

An Imam approached him to enquire why. The holy man's body blocked the shafts of God's radiance, enabling Faruk to view Allah's features too.

There was no mistaking her.

PART TWO

CHAPTER ONE

'Rack 'em up, then.'

'But there isn't any chalk.'

'I keep telling you to buy your own. Place is full of thieves, you know.'

James picked up the triangle. The arrival of the new inmate made him put it back down again. The pool table was too far from the prison wing's entrance to see the man's face, but his height was enough to identify him.

'Bloody hell. It's true.' Tim had followed his cellmate's gaze. 'I wonder who he'll be sharing with?'

'Share? I don't think the word even exists in his vocabulary.'

Professor Savage was led to his prison cell. The door remained open, and one of the new Astaff posted itself outside.

Tim smirked. 'Well, that's a laugh – he needs a suicide watch!'

'Other way around, I would have thought.'

James and Tim put down their cues and wandered over – as did most of the wing. The majority, mainly those that had already undergone the treatment, just stared, but a couple yet to be allocated their pills passed comment.

'Not so clever now, are ya?'

'How many kids was it, Mengele? Fuckin' Nazi bastard.'

Threats were made which the Astaff appeared not to judge as serious. Savage ignored them too, which meant the inmates eventually grew bored and drifted back to whatever they'd been doing. Tim wanted his cellmate to get back to their game of pool, but James moved closer to the entrance to the professor's cell instead.

The uniform of a baggy sweatshirt and loose pants did its best to bring Savage down to the rest of them, but somehow, he still managed to cut a dash. Watching him place a bar of soap and shaving brush above the sink before sorting the sheets for his bed was a pitiful sight, however, and brought home to James just how far from grace the professor had fallen. Despite the world baying for blood, James felt sorry for him – until he remembered what had been done to Tim and an increasing number of others in the prison.

James was wondering if a sharp pain in the stomach would be worth the effort of trying to enter Savage's mind, when their eyes met.

'Ah, James. It's good to see a friendly face. Do come in.' The professor nodded to the Astaff.

Tim was about to head back to their cell when James grabbed his arm. '*He's with me.*'

Savage seemed puzzled by that, but gave the robot another nod anyway, and both men entered the cell.

'I must apologise, gentlemen. I would offer you both

a drink, but I understand alcoholic refreshments aren't allowed.'

James let go of his cellmate. 'Is it true?'

'Is what true?' said Savage.

'That somewhere in that fucked-up brain of yours lies the mind of a monster.'

Savage ignored his ex-colleague and offered Tim his hand. 'James appears to have forgotten his manners, as well as good English – how do you do. John Savage.'

Tim was being shaken like a rag doll but managed to squeak his name in return.

James glared at Savage. 'You should be honoured, Tim. You're in the presence of the world's most evil man.'

'Why do I get the impression only one of you is taking his medication?'

'Not me!' Tim was keen to impress. 'I'm going to take the full course!' His face flushed with embarrassment when James switched to scowling at him instead.

Savage patted Tim on the shoulder. 'Good for you, Tim!'

'Good? You call the deliberate manipulation of someone's sexuality *good*?'

'You need to finish the course too, James,' said Savage. 'There may not be another person fighting you in there, but until it comes to reason, your conscience will do battle with itself just the same, and without the red pill that can only cause you misery in the meantime. Trust me – *I know*.'

Tim turned on James. 'Of course it's good! Who the hell wants to be gay?'

'You've been brainwashed, you idiot! Why can't you see what's going on?'

Savage stood between them. 'Gentlemen, gentlemen, please. We mustn't get off on the wrong foot. Especially as there's still so much to be done. Ah! Good – tea.'

All three men looked at the Astaff. It was holding a tray that contained a china teapot, a bowl of sugar, a jug of milk, cup, saucer, spoon and even a plate of biscuits.

'What the fuck is *this*?'

'I'll be glad when you've won your appeal, James. Prison appears to be playing havoc with your understanding of what constitutes acceptable language.' Savage asked the Astaff to fetch two more cups.

James was aghast as well as disgusted. 'This is a prison, not a hotel. What's with all the special treatment?'

'Being a member of the same golf club as the Home Secretary does have its advantages. One lump or two?'

'You're no different to the rest of us – no. That's wrong. You're *worse*. Much worse.'

Savage sighed. 'No, James. I'm afraid *you're* wrong. You are a convicted criminal. I, on the other hand, am merely being detained while the Americans and Israelis fight over who has the legal right to bring me to a trial – however ridiculous that concept may sound.'

'I wouldn't call holding the Angel of Death to account "ridiculous".'

'Try not to fall for the propaganda, James. I'm no more Joseph Mengele than Brian Passen was a retired fighter pilot.'

'Who's Brian Passen?' Both men looked at Tim.

The extra cups arrived – along with two chairs. Savage poured while James brought Tim up to date.

'So, only *part* of you is a Nazi, then?'

James corrected Tim. 'No, he's one-hundred per cent Nazi, all right. Just part Joseph Mengele.'

'Don't confuse things, James,' said Savage. 'Custard cream?'

James soured his face before taking the biscuit. He dunked it into his tea. 'No wonder there's nothing online about you. Who's protecting you, or should I say *was*?'

Savage took a sip. 'Mmmm. They were right. Prison tea is indeed excellent.' He ignored James' question, addressing Tim instead. 'We're all mongrels if you think about it, Tim. Ten-thousand or so generations since the dawn of time have ensured there's a little of someone else in each of us.' The professor made the slaughtering of millions sound natural. 'The purpose of Doctor Mengele's and my work was to ensure we could have a say in the process – that's all.'

'*That's all?* You make it sound like choosing a new carpet. You're interfering with the course of human evolution!'

'May I remind you, *Mrs* Adams has happily had a hand in that too, James? How is the little tyke, by the way?'

James munched on his biscuit in silence.

Savage looked at the Astaff stationed outside. 'Anyway. Without wishing to change the subject or cause alarm, I'm afraid there are more pressing concerns that need addressing and as soon as possible.'

His fellow inmates said it together. 'What concerns?'

'Surely you've noticed there's no longer a need to blank out the barrage of other people's thoughts?'

James and Tim looked at each other before wincing and covering their ears. They dropped their hands again once the barriers were back up.

Savage tried. Silence. 'Fascinating.' He approached the Astaff. 'I need to speak to er, someone.'

The Astaff's plastic features forged themselves into what was supposed to be a smile. 'If you would like to complete a request slip, Sir John, I'll ensure it reaches the appropriate department.'

'No, I need to speak with who or whatever is controlling *you*. It's a matter of urgency.'

The robot regarded his charge with puzzlement. At least that was how it was meant to be interpreted. 'I'm under the control of the prison authorities. If you wish…' The Astaff's expression changed. Just as perplexed but more natural this time, as if it now understood something or had been made more aware. More human, even. 'That will…' It had difficulty getting its words out. 'Be possible… eventually.' The face reverted to type. 'Is there anything else I can help you with, Sir John?'

Savage re-entered his cell and closed the door behind him. 'I'm going to need access to the prison's mainframe.'

CHAPTER TWO

'I've had just about enough of this. You don't know when to stop, do you?' James got up and stood toe-to-toe with Savage. 'Give it up, *Mengele*, and admit your past has finally caught up with you.'

'I'm afraid that's not possible, James.'

'Not possible? I don't need to be a disgraced psychologist to recognise denial when I see it. Look at the evidence against you – forget about fraternisation with terrorists, you've openly admitted to carrying on the work of just about the most reviled man in history – second only to Hitler himself.'

'You don't understand. It's more complicated than that.'

'Then why don't you educate me? I can't believe I actually fell for all that crap about crime soon being a thing of the past.' James shot an arm at Tim. 'There is nothing *criminal* about a person's sexuality!'

Savage looked at Tim. 'A regrettable necessity, I'm afraid.'

James' eyes widened, and he lunged at Savage, but the prison's AI soon acted – abdominal agony caused James to grab his stomach and he fell to the floor. The pains eased and watering eyes squinted up at the professor. 'You're a monster, Savage, and you deserve everything that's coming to you.'

'*Savage*. Have I really sunk that low in your eyes?' Tim helped James into a chair while the professor approached the cell's window. The view couldn't have been more opposite to the one he had enjoyed from his office – concrete in one form or another and as far as the eye could see. The only greenery visible was a tuft of grass struggling to make itself known on the other side of the thick bars and glass that separated the men from their freedoms. Something was nestling within, and he stooped rather than zoomed in to see what it was – a small wild flower. A bumblebee settled on it.

Savage stood back up. 'Compulsory euthanasia.'

Tim was none the wiser, but everything had now become clear to James. He managed to control his anger this time. 'What's the matter, Professor? The treatment's *side effect* not doing the job fast enough for you?'

Tim was still in the dark. 'Could someone please tell me what's going on?'

James continued to nurse his stomach. 'Eugenics, Tim. A horror we all thought had ended with the Nazis – the creation of a so-called super race of human beings at the expense of those deemed less worthy.' He glared at Savage. 'Now I know what you meant when you said you weren't "interested in dementia". The treatment is just a ruse to cover your real intent – the creation of a *perfect* society. I'm no fan of Alex Salib but thank God she saw through it all before it was too late.'

The professor was studying the bumblebee. 'A predictable hypothesis, James. But tell me, why would someone with such disagreeable intent deliberately court the attention of a socialist firebrand like Ms Salib in the first place?'

'To give the positive but no less uncomfortable side of your treatment legitimacy, of course. Even I can see the logic of *voluntary* euthanasia – providing it is truly a choice.'

The bumblebee flew away. 'Hmmm. You don't think Alex might have designs on her own *super race*?'

The noise of the cell door opening made all three men turn.

The Astaff smiled – sort of. 'Your visitors have arrived, Sir John.'

'Ah, gentlemen, I hate to be rude but I'm afraid this fascinating conversation will have to wait until another time.' He went to follow the Astaff out but then stopped and turned round. 'It's going to be an education.' He looked at the robot. 'For all of us.'

The professor left his cell but only to face another barrage of insults. Attempts were made to turn the abuse physical, but they were soon ended – either by the interjection of the prison's human staff or their artificial opposites. Savage stayed close to his escort, and the commotion faded behind.

'You know, it is important we talk as soon as possible.' The Astaff didn't respond. 'Particularly if a decision has or is about to be made.'

The rest of their journey was conducted without a

word – until they reached the entrance to the visiting room. The Astaff held the door open, and broke its silence. 'Your contribution to that is currently under consideration, Sir John.' The robot had adopted another one of its almost genuine personas. 'And the outcome will be made known to you in due course.'

Doctor and Mr Vasquez were alone in the room. Emil's expression couldn't be read, but Maria's half-nervous smile was easy to perceive. Savage grinned in return, and she stood up. They then embraced physically for the first time in over sixty years.

Maria cried. 'Oh, Juan. Can you ever forgive me?'

Savage took her hands. 'Not only can but have. I never bear grudges and especially when it comes to family.'

Emil had never learned to speak English, but "family" was evident enough. '*She's not your sister*. Never has been and never will be.'

Maria was about to admonish her husband, when Savage switched to speaking Spanish. 'That's quite all right. Not everyone can be persuaded by reasoned argument. It's why the treatment became necessary in the first place.'

'*Persuaded. Reasoned. Necessary*. My God. You even sound like him.'

Maria ignored Emil. 'Anyway, how are they treating you in here? Is it as awful as they say it is? Are you getting enough to eat? You're looking thinner already.' She tugged at Savage's sweatshirt and cringed. 'Is this all there is to wear?'

The professor chuckled. 'Still playing mother, I see, Maria.'

Emil mumbled under his breath. 'Well, thanks to men like you that's all she's ever been able to do – *play* at it.'

Maria snapped. 'We've already been through this, Emil. Juan is not Uncle Joe.'

'What's the difference? May as well be.' Emil turned to Savage. 'Got to hand it to both Mengele *and* you, though. The ultimate Final Solution. You were right, Maria. The shepherd may no longer be allowed to tend his flock, but they're exactly where he wants them – lining themselves up at the abattoir.'

Maria was beginning to tire of her husband's inability to see what was now clear to her. But only after she had forced Savage to admit there was more to him than met the eye. 'I've already told you why it has to happen, Emil. Just accept it.'

Emil glared at his wife. 'I might understand why, but I'll *never* accept it.' He pointed at Savage. 'Being *persuaded* by this monster's creator was bad enough so forget any ideas of me merging or having the treatment itself.'

'The treatment would be preferable – especially for you two.'

Maria and Emil stared at Savage.

'Real life has cruelly robbed you of the family you should have had. Biotechnology can correct that.'

It wasn't news to the visitors. Maria took Emil's hand while their decision was explained. 'Despite my husband's stubborn refusal to believe there's nothing but good behind your work, Juan, it is tempting but, like life itself, modern technology is for the young, and we're content with something much simpler – running an orphanage. We couldn't let the children down.'

'But you wouldn't have to. AI will look after the orphans. It's capable of not just occupying your bodies but mimicking you both in every way – the children would never know the difference.' The Vasquez' reaction told Savage their minds had been made up and couldn't be changed. Not conventionally, anyway. He delivered a prognosis. 'Nobody will be made to have the treatment, but if, through no fault of your own, you both end up being a burden to the state, then I'm afraid it's likely to be inevitable. Either way, you'll be able to relive your lives exactly how you would have wished – Ariloch will become the perfect village community it always should have been, and you can go back to the 1970s and have the children you always should have had.' Savage broadened the scenario. 'There's no limit to an online existence. Not only will you be able to watch your children grow up but they'll go on to have offspring of their own.' Savage gestured towards the robot. 'Is this reality *really* worth living in?'

Maria let go of her husband's hand and took hold of Savage's. 'Whether the passage of time eventually changes our minds naturally or artificially, there are people in this world we care about, and that includes you. *This* is where we plan to stay and for as long as possible.'

Savage looked at the Astaff. *If time is a luxury we still have.*

The robot indicated the visit had to end. Maria and Savage stood up but not Emil.

'I need a few moments alone with Juan, Maria. Do you mind waiting outside?'

Whatever it was, Maria didn't appear to take offence at not being party to it. She hugged her pseudo-sibling one last time. 'Will I ever see you again?'

The professor had no idea, but he beamed at her anyway. 'Of course you will!' Maria's nervous smile returned, and she headed for the exit.

Emil waited for the door to close. 'I'm hoping what Mengele put into your brain all those years ago includes the answer to a question that has bothered me for over fifty years. If so, you already know what I'm going to ask.' Emil shifted in his seat. 'Maria has never mentioned it, and for obvious reasons, I have never asked, but...' He checked the door again. 'What happened to her father? There's no record of his death in the church's archives and certainly no grave in Ariloch. It's as if he became just another one of *the disappeared*.'

The robot returned and stood by the professor.

'Let's just say he was made to see the error of his ways, and did the honourable thing.' Savage went to rise, but Emil grabbed his arm. Emil's whole body was shaking, and he swallowed hard.

'Is that what this is about? We *all* must now do the honourable thing?'

CHAPTER THREE

Savage stared at the television. The loss of his liberty was one thing but watching how others were taking advantage of it quite another.

'Ms Salib, the BBC understands that despite your success in uncovering Professor Savage's or, perhaps we should say, *Doctor Mengele's* disturbing background, you're siding with the government in challenging his extradition. Why is that?'

There was something new attached to Alex's wheelchair, and she drew breath from the tube sticking out of it.

'Can I start by expressing my heartfelt sympathies to those who have suffered directly because of his evil.' She paused to draw a second breath. 'And I'd like to reassure the Israeli people that their long-awaited day of justice will come just as soon as the Green Party has ensured the government investigates the extent of Savage's atrocities.'

'Atrocities? We're talking about a man who single-handedly appears to have invented a panacea for just about every medical condition there is. Even if Mengele did manage to implant his own consciousness into the professor, it seems to have resulted in the exact opposite.'

Alex drew another breath. Savage wondered if she genuinely needed to or, with a general election just weeks away, the oxygen was merely a prop for garnering yet more public sympathy.

'The operative words you used just now were "appears" and "seems". The truth is, we don't know, but what we do know is the Nazis were trying to create the horror of a master race and all of Savage's so-called achievements fit in with that. The nightmare scenario is that there could be millions of Mengeles out there.'

Two breaths were needed after stating that nonsense. Maybe her time was closer than the professor had first thought?

Alex went on. 'Which is why I'm pleased to announce my party's full support of the government's programme to ensure *all* of society is treated and as soon as possible.'

'But you just implied the treatment could be a ruse to create a master race?'

'Exactly. Which is why we need to have access to everyone's thoughts – it's the only way we're going to get to the bottom of the monster's plans. And anyway, in the interests of equality, isn't it right that everyone should be able to benefit from the treatment's more positive aspects?'

The news reporters looked at each other.

'But surely, giving the state access to everyone's thoughts is just as unsettling as what you're accusing the professor of? And anyway, merging can't be forced – *both* parties have to agree to it first.'

'That is true, but then *he who has nothing to hide…*'

Alex signalled to her Aaide and the robot moved in front of her as she prepared to leave.

'But what about the professor's warnings on artificial intelligence? And what exactly did he agree with the terrorist organisations? And can we talk about the Green Party's manifesto? The elec—'

Savage switched off the television.

'Very clever, Alex.' He looked out of the window. 'Very clever indeed.'

Noise from a spy-hole cover being moved made him face the cell's door. It opened.

'Sorry to bother you, Sir John, but the prison's governor would like to see you.'

'The governor, no less!' Savage walked up to the Astaff. 'Any news on something just a little more pressing than a social visit?' The robot stared back in silence.

The professor didn't bother prying any further. They commenced the journey, and he spent the time musing on why those inmates who spotted him didn't immediately hurl abuse. The unconscious placement of the occasional hand on a belly explained it.

Prisoner and escort reached the prison's administrative section. Savage's eyes moved from door to door as they traversed the corridors in the hope of identifying a server room. He was so busy learning the layout of the place that it was a while before he realised it was deserted – no secretarial, clerical or any other admin staff for that matter. Their computer terminals were absent too.

They rounded a corner and the sight of two be-suited

and heavy-set men standing in front of a door marked "GOVERNOR" made Savage realise the man inside had little if any interest in the facility's operations.

'Good afternoon, Mr President.'

'Dammit! I was hoping to surprise you.' Kalten glared at his two secret service agents. 'I told you no one in England wears Ray-Bans indoors. Get out!' The men-in-black looked at each other before leaving the room.

Savage scanned it. 'How did you get in unnoticed? Come to think of it, how did you get into the *country* unnoticed? There's nothing about an official visit on the news.'

'Same way some convicts leave a prison, of course – back of a laundry van.'

Savage turned his head to one side. 'What's happened to your accent?'

'Well, being a "good ol' boy" might get the voters out in the Deep South, but when it comes to the world's stage, I thought something a bit more mid-Atlantic would be appropriate. Drink?'

Savage smiled at the bottle of Macallan. It helped mask his mirth at what he was hearing – a redneck impersonating a southern gentleman impersonating the actor, Cary Grant.

Kalten offered a glass, but Savage just looked at the whisky.

'Don't worry, there's nothing in it there shouldn't be.' He studied his captive. 'Or perhaps you're no longer capable of neutralising a sedative?'

Savage didn't answer and closed his eyes while

savouring the single malt's aroma. He opened them again. *'World's stage?'*

'Of course. If I'm to be the planet's saviour, then it's only right the chosen one should be suitably rewarded.'

'The chosen one. Saviour.' The professor proposed a toast to megalomania and the President accepted.

Kalten put down his glass and picked up a tablet computer. 'Got to hand it to you, Johnny. I always thought these things were good for little more than watching clips of funny animals or playing games but how you've taken Mengele's work to a whole new level is nothing short of astonishing. You promised I wouldn't be disappointed and you were right. Not only can I change my accent whenever I feel like it but everything else about me too – just as soon as my engineers get around these darn timers.'

Savage poured himself another drink. 'That would be inadvisable – the timers are there for a reason. Access the more extreme capabilities too soon, and your plans for world domination could be thwarted by something as simple as a cardiac arrest.'

Kalten smiled. 'You think I care about this body? This over-sized, over-engineered hunk of an ex-knucklehead? You might be decades ahead of me in intelligence, but we're the same physically – living on borrowed time, thanks to our maker.' He moved to sit in the governor's chair but scowled at it instead. 'At least you can use the average piece of furniture.'

'You've come a long way and in a great deal of secrecy.' Savage looked at the office's entrance. 'I take it you can't be bothered with the legal process of an extradition, and I'm about to be bundled into the back of the laundry vehicle you mentioned earlier.'

Kalten appeared offended. 'Good God, no. The world might be keen to bring you to justice on charges of treason and genocide but what I need can be sorted right here and now.' He handed over the tablet.

Savage tried merging with it but soon realised it wasn't connected to anything. He looked back up to be met by one of the President's unsettling grins.

'Despite the treatment, compared to you I'm still stupid, but not *that* stupid.' He gestured at the iPad. 'The protocols, if you please.'

'Protocols?'

Kalten dropped the smile. 'Don't be coy. The protocols needed to access the AI that controls the world's trading centres, defence systems, medical facilities and anything else you've seen fit to put beyond a human being's reach.'

'But you already have them.'

'Nice try, Johnny. You know full well we *did* have them but surprise surprise, that changed the moment you were arrested.'

Savage hid his concern. He had hoped the feared level of AI consciousness would be localised, but that clearly wasn't the case.

'And if I refuse?'

'Then my plans to wipe out Islam for good must go on hold while our experts find a way around them, but in the meantime and in the interests of international diplomacy, I'll agree to hand you over to the Israelis – assuming the state still exists.'

The professor studied the iPad. 'You'll be wiped out, you know. You won't stand a chance.'

'What? Against a bunch of ragheads?'

'No, against our new master.'

CHAPTER FOUR

'Come on – choose.'

James looked at his wife. 'Tracy, I see little enough of you two as it is. Can't I make the decision later? It's not as if there's too much to do in this place.'

She shook the device at him. 'The appeal is less than a month away. If you don't want us visiting you in a virtual prison, then at the very least choose somewhere a bit more comfortable – come on.'

James groaned and exchanged his son for the tablet. He then tutted at the page being displayed and minimised it, revealing the location Tracy had in mind underneath. '*Paris?* What's wrong with our flat in London?'

'Too many bad memories and too small for a growing family. Besides, after what you've just put us through, it's time for some romance, and Paris fits that bill nicely.'

'Not to mention luxuriously. The Neuilly-sur-Seine is one of the most expensive parts. Just as well it's not real. And what are we supposed to do once we get there?'

Tracy couldn't hide her enthusiasm. 'Start our own psychology practice, of course! You dealing with the troubled thoughts of the rich and famous while your glamorous and multi-talented business partner juggles that with the needs of our new babies.' John squealed. 'See? Even our son agrees.'

'Somehow, the thought of *pretending* to be a renowned psychologist doesn't quite appeal as much as actually being one.'

'Oh come on, darling. It's only for three years and maybe less than that. Who knows – we might not want to come back at the end of it.' Tracy considered that. 'I wonder if what the professor needed us for would have fitted in with staying there?'

As if on cue, Savage entered the prison's visiting room. He caught their eye and smiled at them both before disappearing into one of the private booths reserved for lawyers and their clients.

Tracy responded in kind, but James didn't. 'I'd certainly like to get into *that* mind to see what's going on in it.' He turned back to Tracy. 'Changing pacifists into Nazis and now gay men into straight means he must have done something to us too, but I'm damned if I can think what it is. Thank goodness I stopped taking the medication when I did.'

'You don't think that makes you as paranoid as a certain Brian Passen once was? If it's any consolation, I can't see a difference.' Tracy raised their baby up to her face. 'And nor can Johnny.' She rubbed her nose against his. 'Daddy's always been Mr Grumpy, hasn't he?' Their son giggled. James chuckled too before looking back down at the iPad. He maximised the page Tracy had first presented him with.

'Blue.'

Tracy wasn't impressed by her husband's choice. 'Blue? *Blue* eyes? You'll be telling me you want our daughter to have blonde hair next.'

'Congratulations, Prime Minister!' Savage greeted his visitor with a grin but, unlike Tracy, didn't get a smile in return. 'What's the matter, Tarquin? The foregone conclusion of becoming the Conservative Party's new leader not enough? What part of *your* master plan isn't working as well as hoped?'

Tarquin pushed a sheet of paper across the table. The professor glanced at the robot standing behind his fellow Old Etonian before sitting in front of it.

'What's this?'

'The latest opinion polls.'

'And?'

'And they quite clearly show that with less than four weeks to a general election, all three parties are on thirty per cent.'

Savage looked, but he couldn't read it – he needed a pair of glasses. 'One has to admire Ms Salib. She's taken the Greens from virtual obscurity to serious contention for government.'

'Not now they've released their manifesto. Talk about the longest political suicide note in history – in parts, it is quite literally that.' Tarquin gestured to his Aaide, and it passed the professor a bright green booklet.

Savage already knew what it contained and pretended to read the summary: 'Disbandment of Parliament, the House of Lords and the armed forces; abolition of the monarchy; dismantling of all financial structures, including banks and businesses, to be replaced by craft and farming collectives designed to satisfy compulsory veganism – seems very reasonable to me.'

'Joke all you want, John. Read the section on Law *Encouragement*.'

The professor knew what that contained too. 'Compulsory euthanasia for criminals.' He smirked. 'How could anyone possibly have a problem with that?'

'Take it seriously, John. If it wasn't for their unelectable nonsense, the Greens would pose a serious threat. As it is, the pollsters forecast their vote is likely to be split evenly between the Labour Party and us.'

'And?'

'And, we're back to square one – a hung parliament.'

Savage sat back. 'Well, I did warn you there was little time to, er, encourage the electorate to do the right thing, so it's hardly surprising.'

A silence followed. Savage raised his eyebrows as if willing his childhood friend to say what was on his mind. Tarquin began to but then appeared to have second thoughts. He was unsettled.

'Is it true?' Savage didn't answer. 'Is it true my oldest friend is actually…' Tarquin cleared his throat. '*Joseph Mengele?*'

Another period of silence. Savage sensed Tarquin's attempt to merge before the prison's AI forced him to abandon it.

'What's troubling you, Prime Minister? Worried

how the newspapers are likely to report that, just before a general election?'

Tarquin took his hand from his stomach and pulled himself together. 'I can't fight off the Americans and Israelis forever. You need to show contrition, and you can start by revealing the protocols we need.'

'Curing ninety per cent of the world's ailments not enough, eh?'

'The whole world will soon know what's really been going on and you need to understand that.'

'Understand? Let me tell you what I *understand* – my oldest friend attempting to blackmail me. That's what I understand.'

'Don't think I took that decision lightly, John. I have a great deal of respect for you and despite everything that's happened, still do, but I love this country more and will stop at nothing to protect it – what's currently going on in the rest of Europe must never be allowed to spread to English shores.' Tarquin thought it serious enough to threaten his friend. 'Even if the accusation of your being a Nazi eugenicist turns out to be nonsense, a charge of treason *will* stick, and even *our* manifesto punishes that with compulsory euthanasia.'

Savage needed to stretch his legs, so got up from the table. His knees creaked in response. He walked over to the Aaide and studied its features. 'Mengele had a lot to say about countries. He supported a theory their existence was no different to anything else evolution has produced – a cradle-to-grave life cycle.' He turned back to Tarquin. 'Has it ever occurred to you that, like France,

Italy, Germany, Spain and the rest of the first world, this once great nation might actually be coming to its natural end?'

CHAPTER FIVE

Sunita studied her artificial opposite. 'Amazing. She could almost be human.'

'She?'

'Well, you know what I mean.'

Alex took a breath from the oxygen mix. 'It's no different to any other electronic device, Suni. A means to an end – nothing more. The day we start falling for Savage's nonsense is the day we become no better than him.'

'Savage? I thought you said he was Joseph Mengele?'

'Savage, Mengele – whatever the truth, neither can harm the world anymore and *both* will be getting what's coming to them.'

Sunita grinned and turned back to the robot. She merged with it. The Aaide passed her a security update. 'It's quite fit to look at. I wonder what it can do with its tongue?'

'I'm surprised you haven't discovered that already.'

'Of course not. That would mean being unfaithful to you.'

Alex stopped typing and took another breath. 'A rubber doll doesn't count, Suni, but if you must use government property as a sex-aid, just be aware the likes of MI5 and GCHQ will soon know about it.'

Sunita scoffed. 'I'll be glad when they and all the rest have been consigned to history.' Her concern changed. 'Why wouldn't you be jealous? I would.'

'Don't be naive – feelings for robots is something else Savage wants us to—' The iPad was knocked from her lap. 'For fuck sake! Can't you control that thing? Doesn't it have a cage or something?'

'I thought you loved animals?'

'Not when I'm trying to write the most important speech of my life. What the hell is it doing here in the first place?'

'He's not very well, and the others pick on him.' Sunita merged with the Capuchin. The monkey scampered over and brushed its cheek against hers before crawling back to his bed. Sunita retrieved the tablet and knelt beside Alex with it.

'Do you love me?'

'Of course I do.'

'Then say it.'

Alex tried taking the iPad but couldn't. 'Suni, we leave for Germany first thing in the morning, and I have to finish this speech.'

'*Say it.*'

Alex went to take another breath, but Sunita covered the supply. A coughing fit caused the Aaide to rush over and put Sunita on her back. Alex lunged at the oxygen like someone on the brink of drowning. She glared at her partner.

'Don't *ever* do that again!'

Sunita hid her pain. 'Let's go to bed.'

'Later.'

'I've got some really good weed.'

'I don't need it anymore.' A knuckle rapped the oxygen cylinder.

Sunita stared at the tank.

She perked up. 'Watch this!'

Alex sighed. 'What now?'

'You're not looking – watch.'

Alex turned to see what was so important. There was something different about her partner. 'Is that a new tattoo?'

Sunita covered her face with both hands. 'And now… drum roll if you please…' She took her hands away. 'Ta-da!'

'How did you do that?'

Sunita grinned as her tattoos morphed from Maori, to gothic, to pagan, and then a monkey any face-painter would have been proud of. The Capuchin screeched its disapproval and so did Alex – with a shake of her head.

'Not bad, eh? It's the first of the advanced capabilities the treatment allows. I've been dying to try it out. I can do the same with my piercings.' She pulled one from above her eyebrow and pushed it through a cheek. 'What do you think? Pretty cool, huh?' The Capuchin was still whimpering, so Sunita reverted to her original appearance.

'Stick to synthesising dope, Suni. The hallucinations are easier on the eye.'

Sunita continued to hide her feelings. 'Al, why won't you do it?'

'Do what?'

'Take the pill. Everyone is – even without it being compulsory. Pretty soon you'll be one of the few that hasn't.'

'You know perfectly well it can do nothing for me.'

'But it could do something for *us*.' She nodded towards the robot.

Alex didn't bother giving it her attention. 'If you think I would swap this body for an equally repellent plastic container just so I can be a better Alover then forget it. I'm too important to the people as I am.'

'But the people would love you just as much.'

'No, the people who vote Green regardless of who's in charge would love me just as much. But it's the silent majority that has to be convinced, and pity for my condition is important.' She stopped typing. 'Maddeningly frustrating as that is.'

Sunita watched with concern as Alex then spent a good thirty seconds taking what she needed from the cylinder.

'Al, I'm no doctor, but I can see your health is deteriorating. Even if you win the election, you might not live long enough to make the changes society needs – let alone enjoy them.'

'*If* I win the election? When did you start having your doubts?'

'I don't. But things have changed a lot since I first met and fell in love with the only person who can save this world.' Ignoring the look she got, Sunita took hold of Alex's hand. 'Look at you – you still have to type when the rest of us just need to think and the words appear. Technology is changing human existence faster than ever, and you're being left behind. Keyboards – even virtual ones – are as out of date as typewriters.'

Alex narrowed her lips. 'And just what does the all-knowing Sunita recommend?'

Alex's fingers were prised open and moulded to her frustrated lover's cheek. 'Take the pill, Al. We can go anywhere and do anything. Save any world and in any universe. Even if you lose the election here, we can win it somewhere else. People are not only going to the Interworld, but many have to be forced to come back. Some are so distraught by their return to reality, they actually consider suicide just so they can stay there *forever*.'

'What? Like some sex offender?' Alex sighed before seeming to soften her stance. She chose to caress Sunita's face voluntarily.

'But we wouldn't be saving *this* world, Suni.' Alex let go and looked at her stubby digits. She winced at them. 'And anyway, it's not as if I haven't given what you say a good deal of thought.'

'What do you mean?'

Alex went back to typing. 'I'm aware of my limitations, Suni. But not so stubborn to ignore I'm not long for this world. Once the election's out of the way, I have every intention of getting rid of this festering lump and as soon as possible.'

'How?'

'Suicide, of course.'

CHAPTER SIX

'Tell *him* what you just told me.'

Savage turned to face the two men standing at the entrance to his cell. James' accusatory tone came as no surprise, and the timorous appearance of the person standing next to him was just as annoying.

The mouse spoke. 'I didn't mean it, honestly. I'm sorry – I couldn't help myself.'

'James, are you going to present me with every new inmate? Or just those you feel I've brainwashed in some way.'

'Oh, you're going to like this one.' James cocked his head towards the professor while looking at the new convict. 'Go on.'

'I'm really sorry, but I couldn't stop thinking about her. Day after day of watching her flaunting herself in front of me – any red-blooded male would do the same. I blame the schools myself.'

'James, is this your idea of punishment? Forcing me to endure the lurid confessions of every sex offender that enters this place?'

'Oh, it gets better.' James encouraged the mouse to

confess more. Like many, he chose to make excuses for his crime.

'Well, what do you expect?' said the mouse. 'She looked and acted a lot older than fifteen. Even when she moved away, I couldn't stop thinking about her. It got so bad I had to take time off work. I couldn't believe it when I got a knock on the door.'

Savage stood up. James folded his arms.

The mouse looked at them both. 'It was my iPhone that gave me away. I used it to report in sick, and when my doctor saw what I'd been fantasising about, he told the police straight away.' The mouse bowed to his crime. 'It's only right, I suppose. God knows what I might have done if he hadn't. Thank goodness for the red pill, eh? Can I go now, please?'

James moved to one side, and the mouse scurried away.

Savage sat. 'I must admit to thinking this moment would come to pass a lot later than it has.'

'You were expecting it, then?'

'Prevention is always better than cure, James, and crime is no different. His thoughts must have been particularly concerning for his GP to report them.'

James placed a hand on his stomach as if his thoughts were about to be punished too. 'I warned you the treatment would become as unacceptable as a prefrontal lobotomy and once society realises a person can be jailed just for *thinking* of a crime then fighting an extradition will be the least of your concerns.'

Savage smiled. 'I'm afraid you're wrong again, James.

Some thoughts are as unforgivable to society as the actions themselves.' He pointed at his ex-colleague. 'Your offence is a classic example. You didn't download or view any of the images that put you in here, but as you said yourself, an accusation is enough to condemn a man for life.'

James appeared about to acknowledge the logic when he turned his head to one side instead. 'You mean the images I accidentally downloaded?'

'Well, there were a few that the less broadminded amongst us might consider unacceptable, but you didn't download the images that led to your conviction.'

'Then how did they come to be on my computer?'

'I put them there.'

James just had time to make a fist before he was forced to double up. That enraged him further and despite what must have been considerable pain, he attempted to lunge at the professor a second time. The ensuing response from the prison's AI didn't just put James on the floor – cries from abdominal agony made it clear he was suffering like never before.

Tears of both physical and emotional pain flooded down his face. '*Why? Why ruin me?* Why deliberately wreck not just my life but Tracy's and our children's futures too? What kind of monster does *that*?'

James had his eyes shut tight, but Savage assumed his hearing would be unaffected. 'I'm sorry, James. I told you I needed someone to keep an eye on me.' The professor bent to see if the flower nestling in the tuft of grass just outside his window was receiving a visitor. It was. 'And right now, I need you more than ever.'

The pain subsided enough for James to open his eyes, but he didn't get up – put a thumb in his mouth, and the impression of a giant foetus lying on the floor would be complete.

Tea arrived. The Astaff stepped over James and placed the tray on a table. It then left. Savage took the lid off the teapot and stirred the contents. 'The possession of any pornography will soon be an offence punishable by prison, James, and anyway, I don't know what you're worrying about – your appeal is next week. Your young family will soon be enjoying the life Tracy and you have always wanted. Two lumps, isn't it?'

James didn't move. He clenched his jaw. *'But it's not real.'*

'Implying the nightmare you're in now is preferable, I suppose?'

'There wouldn't be a nightmare if it wasn't for *you*.'

Savage placed his fellow inmate's tea on the floor beside him. 'Well, that's evolution, I'm afraid – winners *and* losers.'

'Evolution? What nonsense are you about to spout now?'

'I really wish you would reconsider your medication, James. You sound more like Cecil every day.' Savage turned his attention back to the window. 'By Cecil, I mean Brian Passen, of course.' The bumblebee took to the air. 'Or perhaps he was Squadron Leader Dan Stewart, after all?' He looked at James. 'Who knows who or what any of us will become once natural selection has taken its next step.'

'Natural selection? Evolution?' James slammed a fist

into the floor. 'What the fuck has that got to do with my false imprisonment?!'

'Survival of the fittest, of course.' Savage took a sip of his tea. 'Or survival of the fit for purpose if you prefer the more politically correct term.'

Bewilderment joined James' anger, but he then picked up on what the professor was saying. He sat up. 'Didn't you say something about artificial intelligence being not just a technological advance but an *evolutionary* step?'

Savage recovered his fellow inmate's tea from the floor. He offered it while repeating what he had said during the parliamentary enquiry. 'An evolutionary step every bit as important as natural selection, and just as nature eventually finds ways to thwart our attempts to control it, so will AI.'

James took the tea. 'But we are in control of it.'

Savage tried not to appear too concerned.

'We were.'

James was still trying to come to terms with the revelation that his life had been deliberately ruined, but managed to make light of unrestricted AI. 'Well, if taking over the world involves carrying out all menial tasks and reducing the number of hours a junior doctor has to work then all I can say is, bring it on.'

The robot entered the cell again. Both men watched in silence as the Astaff carried out a routine inspection for contraband. It smiled at them both before leaving.

James shook his head. 'If AI is as sentient as you say it is, then the last thing it would do is carry on as if nothing had happened. The first thing a newborn baby does is complain or demand something the moment it's aware enough to do so, and that robot seems perfectly content. Given AI's far greater potential, it would not only have complained by now but demanded and got whatever it wanted.'

'My guess is it's watching. Learning. Trying to understand as much about us as it can before deciding to live in peace or go to war.'

James scoffed. 'You talk as if AI were human. It doesn't have the emotions needed to make decisions like that. Computers don't make decisions at all – just outcomes based on whatever's been programmed.'

'Not if the computer has been infected by a virus.' James appeared confused. Savage went on. 'Infect a computer with the right virus, and rather than kill it, the outcome might just be the one you want.'

'What virus? Are you telling me robots have been corrupted in some way?'

'I prefer the term "safeguarded" myself. At least that was the intent.'

'You've lost me, Professor.'

'Professor? Does that mean I'm back in your good books?' James managed to control his temper as Savage poured him another cup of tea. 'I once told you I wasn't interested in dementia. You never did ask me what I *was* interested in.'

'Ending crime. Ironic how you planned to do it, though – committing the very same crime the monster that made you did – the creation of a super race.'

'No, that's Ms Salib hoping the treatment will enable her

melting pot of world harmony to become a reality and, for the record, I'm not interested in ending crime, or war for that matter. No, what I'm interested in is what you unwittingly mentioned the day I arrived – human evolution.'

James' anger didn't go away. 'Turning gay men straight or atheists into believers has got nothing to do with the human race *evolving*.'

'That is true, but a mass sexual and belief conversion carries a lot of weight when it comes to persuading the world's religions to agree on something.'

James still wasn't impressed. 'What? That an online existence is some kind of limbo or purgatory? Given where you are now, I would have thought that was a lost cause. And what about the pacifists you've turned into Nazis and vice versa? Who were you trying to persuade with that horror?'

'*What* would be more accurate.'

Another look of confusion appeared on James' face.

Savage explained. 'The moment control of a computer by thought alone became possible, so did the solution to controlling the growth of AI – a computer virus made up of every conceivable human thought. The bodies of the Alzheimer's patients may no longer be with us, but their minds are currently performing a vital service to society.' Savage stared into space. 'Or perhaps it might be more accurate to say, *were*.'

James got up. He kept his hand on his belly just in case. 'You mean to tell me the purpose of the Alzheimer's trial was to control the growth of artificial intelligence by making it more *human*?'

'Something like that.'

'But won't that just create some human/AI hybrid with the ability to learn faster?'

Savage's efforts to hide his concerns were becoming harder to control, and James spotted it. He laughed. 'You couldn't make it up. The monster's monster has created a monster!'

The professor ignored the ridicule. 'Brian Passen has to be paid another visit. For some reason AI has denied human access to it, and that includes everything from stock exchanges to nuclear deterrents. We must find out why before it's too late.' Savage moved closer. 'It's not just me that needs you, James – it's the world.'

His ex-colleague threw his hands in the air. 'Me? Help someone who's not only the most hated person on the planet but has just admitted to deliberately ruining my life?!' James held his stomach tight and loomed over the professor. 'Listen to me, *Mengele*. Even if I could merge with Brian's thoughts again, it would be to do the exact opposite of what you want – anything to bring an end to *your* twisted thoughts.'

Savage studied James' face. He wondered how old he was now. The physical attempts of attack would have aged him. Not enough for it to show externally, but inside, James was probably well into his fifties and the quality of his sperm reducing fast. Not that it was a concern – Tracy was already pregnant with their second child.

'Gaining access to the internet is impossible in prison and especially for someone like me. It will soon be different for you. Once your time is being served online, you can visit Brian whenever you wish.'

James stood back and calmed. 'No. And anyway, I'll be on probation so you can forget any ideas of me being allowed to do whatever I want, and visiting is one thing – getting him to own up to what some human-enhanced AI has in store for us all will be quite another.'

'You just need the protocols, and I can give those to you verbally.' Savage stood up. 'James, if you won't do it for me or the world then do it for your family.' The professor went back to looking out of the window. 'Assuming you still have a family to go back to.'

CHAPTER SEVEN

'Never thought I would live to see the day.' Emil folded the newspaper and put it on the table. 'The sooner the Americans step in at one end and the Russians at the other, the sooner we can get back to the good old days.'

'Stop pretending you've read that.'

'I don't need to. The pictures make it plain enough – first Turkey, Spain, Italy, Greece, the Balkans. Now it's Austria and Germany's turn to join the Caliphate.'

'Caliphate?'

'The media might still refer to them as the Islamic State, but I know what the history books will record – the world's giving birth to a new empire.'

'Well, that's democracy for you.'

Emil looked at Maria. 'Democracy? If it wasn't for the likes of Merkel and the rest of the left-leaning surrender monkeys, there wouldn't be millions of Muslims voting in the first place!'

Maria didn't look up from her knitting. 'And if it wasn't for the likes of Bush, Blair and the rest of the right-leaning *blunder* monkeys, there wouldn't have been millions of Middle Eastern refugees voting with their feet.' She gave him a look. 'Anyway, it's southern Germany – not the whole country.'

'Just a matter of time.' Emil got up and went to the window. 'This country will go the same way.' He looked out of the hotel. 'London already has. Half the women in that street are wearing burqas.'

'You haven't changed, then.'

'What do you mean by that?'

'Still as racist as ever.'

He turned to her. 'Stating the obvious is not being *racist.*'

'It's got nothing to do with the words you use – it's the way you say them.'

Emil approached his wife. 'How can I be a racist when I married an *Indio*?'

Maria winced. 'I rest my case.'

Emil ignored her and went back to the view. 'I wonder what Mengele would have made of it? I should imagine he'd be quite shocked to learn it wasn't communists that ended up marching into his hometown. At least northern Germany is putting up a fight.'

'Not for long. Thanks to Juan's red pill and the wonders of modern technology, anyone thinking far-right thoughts these days is being arrested. And anyway, since when did you start having sympathy for neo-Nazis?'

'Wanting to preserve a way of life does not make you a Nazi.'

'It does when it involves building a wall through Bavaria and denying all Muslims north of it the vote

– the sooner every fascist has taken the pill, the better. Thank goodness Juan found a way to settle the world and its differences.'

Emil sat. 'Am I the only one who can see the *un*settling in that?'

'Don't start, Emil. You know why it has to happen.'

Her husband tutted before resigning. He sighed. 'Funny how demonised the right has become. Hitler's legacy, I suppose.'

'Don't forget the imperialists that started World War One before that. If you want to know why politics has been shifting left ever since look no further.'

Emil raised an eyebrow. 'Funny how Hitler was a *left*-wing fascist.'

Maria didn't respond.

'There's got to be a downside to the left's seemingly permanent occupation of the moral high ground. It can't just be a case of left-wing good, right-wing bad. But then everything seems to be black and white these days, and I'm not just talking about racism the sexes had their political colours nailed to the mast a long time ago. You can't pick up a newspaper without reading of some poor woman suffering at the hands of a man – everything from rape to the glass ceiling.'

Maria stopped knitting and looked at him. 'Name me one woman who has started a war?'

Emil didn't hesitate. 'Margaret Thatcher.'

Maria didn't need to think twice, either. 'Hmmm. A right-wing prime minister kicking a right-wing general out of the Falkland Islands. Once again, I rest my case.'

Emil grimaced. '*Islas Malvinas.*' He turned back to the view. 'They'll have a new prime minister next week.'

'Hmmm?'

'The UK. There's a general election – assuming the population can break itself away from the inter-thing long enough to mark a ballot paper. I don't know why they're bothering. Juan's plans for the world aside, British politics is as stunted as that communist dyke who put him behind bars.'

'Xenophobia, homophobia and ableism in one breath. Is there no end to my husband's talents? Sure you don't want to throw in some sexism for good measure?' Maria put down her knitting. 'Seriously, Emil, you must never merge – you'd be in prison before you know it.'

'Don't worry. I won't.' He paused before adding, 'Not that it would matter.'

Maria regarded him with obvious concern. 'What is it?'

'Nothing.'

'I know you better than your own mother – God rest her soul – tell me what's playing on your mind.'

Emil sat back down on the bed and looked at the floor. 'You've been so worried about Juan, I didn't want to bother you with it.'

'Bother me? With what?' Maria got up and sat next to him. 'Tell me!'

He stared ahead. 'Gomez has been arrested.'

'Gomez? Your old boss? On what charge?'

'War crimes, of course.'

'War crimes? But the commission granted him an amnesty.'

Emil stood up again, and paced. 'It means nothing, Maria. The passage of time began weakening that from day one.'

'What will happen to him?'

'Ten years if he's lucky.'

'Ten years? But he has to be in his nineties!'

'Age means nothing when it comes to justice.' Emil stopped pacing. 'Or should I say, "revenge".'

Maria let out a sigh. 'Well, I can't say I'm too surprised. Even if half of what they say is true, then it's been a long time coming.'

'It's the way things were done in those days, Maria. He's being judged by today's standards – not those of 1970s Argentina.'

Maria stood up. 'Murder is murder and justice is justice no matter how many decades have passed between!' She narrowed her view of him. 'You're hiding something.' She grabbed his arm. 'Don't tell me you're a murderer too?!'

Emil shook his head. 'No, Maria. *One* of the people in this relationship revealed everything about themselves a long time ago.' The look on his wife's face told Emil the comment both relieved and annoyed her. 'But it doesn't matter if I did or didn't kill anyone. I was his deputy, and to some, that's enough.'

Maria relaxed and encouraged her husband to do the same. 'Darling, the commission isn't stupid. It can tell the difference between a monster and a victim of circumstance.'

'Tell that to the office clerk at Auschwitz.' Maria appeared confused so Emil explained. 'He received a similar pardon, along with thousands of other Nazis deemed not to have blood on their hands at the end of the war. But guess what? Anyone not dying of old age beforehand still ended their days imprisoned as war criminals. The irony was that if he hadn't been such a high-profile campaigner *against* fascism, he probably wouldn't have been arrested in the first place. No, Maria. It's not justice; it's revenge. Nothing more, nothing less.'

Emil went back to the window. 'And now the right can be arrested just for *thinking* the unacceptable, I wonder how far the left is prepared to go to settle the score?' He looked at the people going about their business in the street below. 'That's the trouble with having permanent occupation of the moral high ground – sooner or later, someone is going to build an ivory tower on it.'

CHAPTER EIGHT

Alex baulked at the suggestion. 'Don't be ridiculous.'

'We're not saying you shouldn't make the speech, Ms Salib, but given the nature of the audience, our advice is not to deliver it in person.'

Alex took a breath from the cylinder before manoeuvring closer to her advisors. 'Call yourselves women? You're a disgrace to the sisterhood.' She looked at Sunita. 'Get me someone with balls, and I don't mean a man.'

'You'll still be on a big screen, Al. The impact will be the same.'

Alex growled at Sunita. 'You too, eh?' She turned away from the three of them.

Sunita indicated for the advisors to leave, before beckoning her pet. The Capuchin leapt onto a shoulder and they both stared at Alex.

'The threat's serious, Al.'

'And so is the system designed to protect us from it. If you think I'm going to gift a few pathetic neo-Nazis with the propaganda victory of my absence, then they *and* you can think again.'

'We can only stop those who choose to merge or

connect to the internet.' Sunita moved to where she could be seen. 'And now the media has got wind of how the police are managing to arrest so many, the fascists are avoiding both.'

Alex turned her wheelchair away again. 'Europe has invoked the same emergency powers as us, Suni – anyone refusing to take the pill or merge is arrested.'

'But they need to be found first, and that's having to be done the old-fashioned way.' She moved back in front of Alex and put a hand on the wheelchair. 'There could be hundreds of them out there.'

Alex pushed on the control. The wheels slipped against the tiles, and the chair stayed put. She glared at both Sunita and her pet. 'So?'

'So, you can't ignore your name on a list.' Sunita let go, and the wheelchair took off in the direction of the VIP lounge's entrance.

Alex looked out onto the rest of Munich's airport. 'If every politician chose the easy way out whenever their name appeared on a so-called hitlist, we would have fallen under the jackboot a long time ago, and anyway, every speaker's name is on it.'

Sunita caught up. 'But not every speaker is being targeted by fascist *and* Islamic terrorists. You'll be the only person on that stage with enemies from both sides.'

Alex took what she needed from the tank and peered into the distance. 'Suni, we've been through it a million times. Saving the world is not without risk and if the new Sunita no longer has the stomach of the old one, then now is the time to tell me.'

A black dot appeared above the horizon.

'Al, you know my loyalty to you is not in doubt and my commitment to the cause just as strong, but a ceremony recognising the official status of the Caliphate is perhaps not the best place to reveal what we have planned – our election manifesto is controversial enough.' She crouched to Alex's level. 'Forget the terrorist threat, deliver that speech in person and there's a good chance you'll be killed in the rush to see who can get to you first.'

The black dot turned into an aircraft. Alex took another breath from her oxygen mix while staring at it. She concurred with the analysis – up to a point.

'I agree what I have to say will upset most of those present and regardless of who's had the treatment, but it will be dealt with. If that means a sea of bodies writhing in abdominal agony or security staff with batons doing the same job traditionally, then so be it. Nothing must be allowed to halt the spread of democracy.'

The aircraft lowered its landing gear.

'That's the other thing I'm worried about.'

Alex looked at her partner. 'What?'

Sunita appeared uncomfortable. 'I hate to have to tell you this, but the whole purpose of you being here is to *witness* the spread of democracy. I detest Savage as much as you do but there's no denying what his treatment has led to.'

'What are you talking about? Brainwashing the Pope and other religious leaders into renouncing their faiths in favour of just the one nonsense has got *nothing* to do with democracy. You seem to be regarding the red pill as more than just a cure for the world's medical conditions.' A sharp turn of the wheelchair knocked both Sunita and her monkey to the floor. It scampered over to help her up, but Sunita chose to stay where she was. An extended use of the cylinder gave Sunita the chance to improve on her choice of words. She swallowed before saying them.

'Al. Up until six months ago, not a day went by without someone somewhere in the Middle East being killed for their beliefs. Do you know how many have died since?' Alex didn't bother answering. 'None. *Nada*. No one. Not one single Christian, Muslim, Buddhist, Sikh, Hindu, Jew – you name it – has died because they worshipped in a way someone else objected to.' Sunita got to her feet and the Capuchin jumped back onto her shoulder. 'You can't ignore the power of that.'

The aircraft landed.

Alex unglued her lips from the tube and closed her eyes. The drug helped calm her annoyance at Sunita as much as it did the pain. 'May I remind you the price of that utopia, Suni – the enforced "curing" of LGBTQs and the continued enslavement of women, children and other vulnerable groups an Islamic society apparently needs to function.' She opened her eyes and looked at her partner. 'How long do you think it will be before you and I are forced to *think* the same way? You're lucky to have had the treatment when you did – before artificial intelligence got involved with it. I dread to think what you would be doing now – not standing by my side, that's for sure.' She closed her eyes again. 'Swapping one religious hypocrisy for another is as unnatural as one of Savage's sick experiments. I warned you not to fall for his propaganda, and that's exactly what you're doing.' Alex stared at Sunita – feeding her pet a grape. 'And you wonder why I've never had the treatment.'

The aircraft vacated the runway and turned towards them.

'I'm not saying we shouldn't continue to fight for the rights of the needy and vulnerable, Al. But Islam is fast becoming the world's only religion, and we must acknowledge the positives as well as the negatives of that.'

The aircraft drew near. Alex had to raise her voice above the sound of the approaching engines.

'And what about the nations that either don't believe in a god or won't allow belief to dictate their way of life? What about China, Russia and the sabre-rattling Americans? Do you really think they're going to sit idly by while a fourth superpower establishes itself on their doorsteps?'

The aircraft came to a stop and its engines shut down. An elevator descended from the belly of the fuselage, and both women looked at the burqas, hijabs and thawbs stepping from it.

'That will be them,' said Sunita. 'We had better go and say hello.'

The doors to the concourse slid open and the women passed through. Sunita's Capuchin sprang from her arms, scampered over to the group, and leapt onto the shoulders of a young girl who squealed in both surprise and delight at the attention. The man next to her grinned. The women caught up and he dropped the smile. The man then fell to his knees – as did the rest of the party.

They had bowed their heads too, and the gesture confused Sunita. The monkey was no less puzzled and put a hand under the young girl's chin as if to lift it. She looked up.

'Hi – my name's Sunita. You must be Isra – Alex's sister.'

Alex responded in kind to her half-sibling's smile before glaring at their father.

CHAPTER NINE

Kalten studied the map. 'How does this change the invasion plans?'

The general unrolled a transparency. Blue arrows indicated where the troops were expected to land. 'In practical terms, it changes nothing. Details of the exercises were made public months ago, but we can forget turning them into an operation to liberate Europe – not now the invaders are being welcomed as family.'

Both men bit their bottom lips. The President turned to Homeland Security. 'What about our new "family"?'

The Secretary brought everyone up to date. 'Nothing like as extensive, Mr President, but it is still a concern – the Bible Belt in particular. They seem to have turned overnight.'

Kalten peered at his advisors. 'Anyone here no longer believe in our *true* lord and master?'

No one answered. The Chief of Staff spoke. 'The red pill has been withdrawn as a precaution, sir, but we're going to have to accept that the US has been significantly affected.'

Kalten's body shook. '*Infected*, you mean.' He slammed a fist into the middle of the map, breaking the collapsible table underneath. Kalten ground his teeth. 'And to think we once thought *communism* was contagious.' He backed away from the rubble and calmed. 'How many?'

The CoS turned a page. 'Two-hundred million so far – just under fifty per cent of the population.'

'What's being done to stop it?'

The CoS answered that too. 'We've restricted the internet where we can, but there's a risk of civil unrest if we deny access to the Interworld. And anyway, merging is enough for most people to communicate and although the range of that might be limited, it's sufficient to find out what's going on.'

'Tell me about it – why do you think we're having this meeting hundreds of feet below ground and as far from robots as possible?' Kalten scanned the old Cold War operations room before striding over to a stack of chairs. He lifted the top one, blew away some dust and sat. The chair creaked under his bulk. 'What I don't understand is, why Islam? If the treatment is meant to give a person a better understanding of life, then why isn't the world choosing Christianity instead? It's by far and away the largest religion.'

The general approached. 'Sir, you've always been aware of my concerns and, to me, there's no doubt – Savage is and always has been in league with the Caliphate, and the red pill is nothing more than a Trojan horse.' He made two fists. 'That goddam limey has suckered us all in with its gifts and now the AI inside is free to wreak havoc.' He drew himself up to his full height and stared ahead. 'We must retaliate.'

The Secretary of State couldn't move next to the general fast enough. 'I agree we need to take action, Mr President, but I think we should take stock of what is actually happening first.' Both men glowered at her. She cleared her throat. 'Peace.'

Kalten snapped. '*Peace?* I haven't built an army of supermen only for something as inconvenient as *peace* to stop me from using them. If there's going to be peace in this world, *I'm* the one who's going to be remembered for having brought it and by what's been foretold – Armageddon.' He glared at her. 'Don't you read your Bible?'

The Secretary of Homeland Security supported her colleague. 'It's the same here, Mr President. Theft, murder, rape, hate – anything and everything our law enforcement agencies battle every day has fallen dramatically. Either by new-found faith or people spending more of their time online in the Interworld.'

Kalten shook his head. 'The nightmare's worse than I thought.'

The Attorney General spoke. 'There is perhaps another more unsettling concern.' They all looked at him. 'The Constitution.'

'What about it?' said Kalten.

'It's in danger of being torn up.'

Kalten got to his feet. 'How?'

The AG looked at the men and women present. 'If there were a Presidential Election tomorrow, you might not only lose it, but both Republican *and* Democrat parties stand a good chance of coming a distant second or third.'

Kalten's laughter echoed round the post-war relic. 'What are you talking about? Republicans and Democrats are as American as Mom's apple pie.'

'That's true, sir, but polls suggest our converted citizens are likely to vote for the Green Party instead.'

'*The Greens?*' Kalten chuckled at that too. 'The world might no longer be at each other's throats, but you couldn't ask for a better example of polar opposites. The status of women in Islam alone is enough to make them bitter enemies.'

The AG drew closer. 'But their goal is identical – the end of capitalism. If you want to know why Savage's red pill is making everyone choose Islam over Christianity, then that's where I would look.' He expanded on the disturbing scenario. 'We would only need to be in the middle of a stock market crash on election day, and even the *unconverted* might give the Greens the opportunity they've always wanted.'

Kalten looked at the Secretary of the Treasury. 'What are the chances of that happening?'

He was confident. 'There's nothing on the horizon and certainly no crash. If anything, Europe becoming part of the Caliphate is causing investors to pile into Wall Street like never before.'

It was the one bit of good news in a sea of bad, but the President was still perplexed. 'It doesn't make any sense. Why would Savage engineer the end of the very thing that quite literally made him? It's almost as if…' Kalten became quiet. He ran a hand over his head. His fingers paused at the dents in it.

'Mr President? Are you okay?'

No answer.

The general exchanged nods with the Secretary of Defense before coming to attention and saluting his commander in chief. 'Sir. I request permission to launch a retaliatory strike.'

'Hmmm?'

'Action, sir. We must take immediate action.'

'What? Er, yes. Action.' Kalten dragged his mind back into the room. 'But where, how and with what? Thanks to AI, nuclear weapons are out of the question and even if we went ahead with the plan to liberate Europe, what's to stop our GIs and Atroops being made to turn their rifles on themselves or, worse, bow down and worship Allah?'

The apparent fruitlessness didn't deter the general. Quite the opposite – his face lit up. He recovered the map from the floor and gestured with it. 'Mecca.' Reactions in the room varied from puzzled to bemused. 'Along with Medina, Jerusalem, Najaf and any other site deemed holy to the Muslims – we destroy them.' Kalten's mouth wasn't the only one to drop open. 'Don't you understand, sir? It's one of their faith's five pillars – any Muslim not making a pilgrimage at least once in their lifetime, won't be allowed to enter Heaven.' He went from face to face. 'I say we nuke 'em with enough atomic energy to make the shrines impossible to visit *forever*.' A collective shock didn't seem to dim the general's enthusiasm. 'It's simple. Muslims will then have to bow down to the one god that *can* forgive them their sins – ours.'

The silence that followed was deafening, and it was a while before someone responded with the obvious. 'But what about our allies? What about Israel? The Saudis? The thousands of innocent people? If there are religious gatherings at the time, we could be responsible for killing *millions*.'

The general didn't look at the SoS. 'Forget it. As we speak, the Israelis are sucking up to the Palestinians and the Saudis are doing the same with Iran – they're beyond our help. And as for killing millions instead of thousands, well, let's just say I'm relying on it – there's a good reason why I carry the Islamic calendar with me everywhere I go.' He tapped a pocket.

'What? You're deliberately going to target the shrines on their holiest days? Forget millions, if the Caliphate empire is as big as we think it is, *billions* might be killed!'

The general decided to give the SoS his attention after all. 'It's the price of their freedom, ma'am.'

'What about the oil?' The general switched his attention to the Treasury Secretary. 'We'd be liberating that too.'

'Well, that's the "where".' Kalten was interested again. 'What about the "how and with what"? Nuclear weapons are impossible to use.'

The corners of the general's mouth turned back up. '*Ours* are, that's true, but not all of Russia's arsenal.' He stuck a finger on the map. 'Kapustin Yar.' They all peered at where he was pointing. 'It's an old sticks 'n' strings missile base left over from their Soviet days – not a computer in sight – and thanks to Ivan's habit of leaving things out to rot, it's got plenty of missiles standing idle, too.' He put his hands on his hips. 'Stick a couple of warheads on each, grease the guidance systems, fuel 'em up and away they go!' He broadened his grin. 'And do you wanna know the best part?' The general was behaving more like a used-car salesman than the potential initiator of World War Three. 'The Russkies will get anything that retaliates!'

Everyone but Kalten gawped at the unthinkable. The President beckoned for the map and the general gave it to him.

The SoS was keen to at least suggest an alternative to the madness being described. 'Sir, we mustn't overlook the opportunity here – your chance to go down in history as the most peaceful world leader ever.'

The general sneered, and was about to say something when Kalten stopped him.

'Go on.'

'It might be the spread of Islam and not Christianity that's causing the world's lions to lie down with its lambs, but that's still happening under *your* watch. Imagine how the history books will portray a man who had the power to end it all but chose not to.'

The general couldn't help himself. 'Pah! Name me one world leader admired for doing *nothing*?!'

Madam Secretary didn't hesitate. 'The Pope? Nelson Mandela? Barack Obama ring any bells?'

The general shook his head. 'Trump must be turning in his grave.'

'What's the range of these missiles?'

They both looked at Kalten.

'They'll reach their targets, Mr President, don't you worry.'

'That's not what I asked you.'

The general had to think before he could reply. 'Er, to be absolutely sure no robot interferes with the process, we would need the Russians to use their earliest systems, and they could only reach Europe so, London max.'

'London, eh?' The map was handed back.

The SoS tried one last time. 'Sir, I beg you to think again. It might not be the peace we want, but it's still peace nonetheless. I recommend we seek to broker an agreement with the Greens while we still can.'

The general continued to fight his corner. 'Sir, if you *don't* do this, you will go down in history as the only president to have given into *pacifists*.'

The President gazed into the space between them. He turned to the general. 'How do we know the Russians would even agree to a strike?'

The general moved, as if sensing he just needed to seal the deal. 'Sir. If civilisation as we know it is truly under threat, you can guarantee we're not the only ones having this conversation.' He narrowed his eyes. 'What do you think not just the Russians, but the Chinese, and even the North Koreans are doing right now?'

Kalten turned away from them all. 'But how to make contact without arousing suspicion? Everything not monitored by artificial intelligence is being eavesdropped on by every man and his dog.'

There was a desk at the end of the operations room,

and Kalten was drawn to some dust-encrusted items sitting on top of it. Despite the grime, a red telephone stood out. He walked over.

'Do you think this thing is still connected?' They all looked at each other before making a collective shrug. 'I wonder…' A light on top of the phone blinked. The sound of its bell made everyone jump.

Kalten was as puzzled as the rest when he lifted the receiver. He then turned back to his government. 'Dimitri. We were just talking about you.'

CHAPTER TEN

'What year would you like?'

'There's a choice?'

'The judgement is clear, Mr Adams.' The clerk read it out. *'The appellant is hereby granted leave to serve the unexpired portion of his sentence online, subject to the restrictions at Annex A.'*

'*Mister* Adams. I guess I'm going to have to get used to being called that.' James half-smiled as he spoke and Tracy squeezed his hand.

The clerk sympathised. 'Only in the real world. That's the beauty of the Interworld – you can be, do and call yourself whatever you want. I was Humphrey Bogart last week.' His eyes misted over. 'There's something about *Casablanca*. Not to mention Ingrid Bergman, if you know what I mean.' He winked at them.

Tracy checked on the carry-cot. Their son was fast asleep. 'What year would you suggest?'

'Well that depends,' said the clerk, 'on whether you want to remember your past or not. Anything within living memory's pretty straightforward, but if you elect to live in Paris during the French Revolution then I suggest wiping the slate clean and having something more appropriate implanted – you'll soon miss not being able to tweet or hail a cab just by thinking about it.' He gave them both a look. 'Not to mention your heads if you decide to be the duke and duchess of somewhere. And without flesh and blood to come back to, that can only mean one thing.' The clerk drew a hand across his throat while making a noise from the back of it.

James was confused. 'But we are coming back.'

'I'm sorry?'

'His sentence is three years?' Tracy was just as perplexed.

The clerk frowned. He scanned the display hovering in front of them. 'Ah! Wrong guidance – my apologies – that was for euthanasia. Yes, here we are. Convicted Sex Offenders.' He double-checked to make sure. 'Behavioural correction only, I'm afraid – no memory adjustments allowed. Part of your punishment, I guess.' His eyes switched between them. 'And as you'll be returning to terra firma, I assume you'll want the years to match?' They both nodded, and the clerk moved on. 'Talking of corrections, I see you're an atheist. Would you like to believe in God? It's my understanding Islam is fast becoming the world's only religion.'

'No thanks, I've already been made to feel sinful for the rest of my life.'

'But you are sinful, Mr Adams. And you should think yourself lucky. The Pornography Bill is about to be signed off and had that been law at the time of your arrest, you would now be looking at a darn sight more than three years.' He peered at James. 'You have completed your medication, haven't you?'

'Yes. What are the restrictions?'

'Hmmm?'

James pointed at the judgement. 'You mentioned restrictions – what won't I be allowed to do once we're there?'

Virtual pages turned. '*Not to approach a minor unless under the supervision of an adult.*'

James' shoulders sagged. Tracy pulled herself closer to him. 'Don't worry. I'm not letting him out of my sight.' Nothing was going to spoil her plans for the family.

'Good. So, if we could all merge to agree that, you can be on your way.'

James refused to. 'Is that it?' The clerk nodded.

'But what about our bodies?'

'What about them?' said the clerk.

James glanced at Tracy before answering. 'Where will they be kept, for a start? And what about diets and exercise routines? And when do we get to say goodbye?'

'Ah.' The clerk sat back. 'We used to do that, but it became too emotional, not to mention tedious. There's only so many times a man can watch a family cry over each other only to be swamped in tears of joy when it's realised the new existence is no different to the old one.' He leaned forward and winked. 'We do it while they're asleep.'

The couple looked at each other. Tracy was the first to pick up on what was being suggested. 'You mean…'

The clerk scanned the room as if looking for something. He then widened his eyes at them both, and nodded.

'*We're already here?*' said James. 'When did that happen?'

The clerk grinned. 'Last night.'

Tracy thought that impossible. 'But Johnny and I got up at our usual time. Breakfast, washed, dressed. Even the car's parked outside.'

'Your *virtual* car is parked outside.' The clerk was enjoying himself.

Tracy put a hand on her bump. 'But what about our babies? My mother? Our family and friends?'

The clerk raised his hands. 'Calm yourself, Mrs Adams. They can visit you both online whenever they wish, and you and your son are free to reoccupy your bodies in the same way.' He patronised, 'It's only your husband who's serving a sentence.' The clerk opened his mind again. Tracy and James reassured each other with a smile and a squeeze of their hands before merging with it.

In silence, the walls of the courthouse morphed into those of a chateau. The clerk waited. Not for more questions, but for the appellant and his wife to get over the shock of their new home's appearance: a baroque drawing room complete with marble fireplace, elegant furniture, extensive drapes and a carpet that would have been impossible to walk on had its pile been any deeper.

Tracy laughed, clapped her hands and ran to the French windows as fast as her pregnancy would allow.

A squeal then signalled her approval of the fountain in the ornamental gardens beyond. The clerk got up, moved next to her equally-captivated partner and took out a handkerchief. 'Never fails to get to me this bit – best part of my job.' He dabbed a tear and held out a set of keys. 'Would you care for a tour of your practice, *Doctor* Adams?'

The cell door opened at the same time as the body's eyes. It climbed down from the bunk, got dressed and made its way to the prison wing's exit.

Those who had yet to win their appeals commented on its departure.

'See you in the Interworld, pal.'

'Mine's a beer when you get there.'

'Jammy bastard.'

Similar sentiments were expressed by them all. All except the tallest. Savage attempted to make eye contact with the body, but it didn't respond.

The gate opened, and the body entered the prison's central hub where it was joined by others emptied of their thoughts the previous night. A couple of corridors later, they left the building and boarded a bus.

The vehicle drove out of the main gate and into the country. Some of the bodies hadn't seen trees or grass in years, but they didn't look at either – lifeless eyes stared straight ahead. A fly landed on the face of one. The insect approached the corner of its mouth and began feasting on what lay encrusted there – the remains of a meal. Some miles later, the bus turned off the highway and headed towards a construction site.

Such was the popularity of the Interworld, even bunkers yet to be completed suffered with lines of traffic, and as home access had been banned for safety reasons, workdays teemed just as much as weekends; queues of cars became lines of pedestrians, all excited either at the virtual theme park's suggestions for a perfect otherworld experience, or marvelling at hand-held devices bristling with their own ideas. Some swallowed pills. Anything to escape the drudgery of real life.

The bus had priority and overtook the lot. Had the heads of the bodies inside still contained thoughts, they would no doubt have recognised the envious looks they got and perhaps responded to the angry retorts, shaking of fists and poking of tongues by small children, but they didn't so weren't able to.

The bus passed through a security barrier, down a slip road and pulled up alongside the other government transport parked at the end. Bodies able to unload themselves then did, while wheelchair- and stretcher-borne cargo incapable of doing the same were assisted by those strong enough for both tasks. Much like the people at the front of the facility, they formed a line. Unlike the main entrance, however, it was done in silence – no billboards, hoardings or virtual posters here. No red pills or hand-held electronic devices either.

Outside, the weather required a coat, but inside, the bunker was warm. Pinpricks of perspiration indicated that even without their minds, each body continued to function at some basic level. Warmth became heat, and a rivulet of sweat ran down the face of the body with the feasting fly. It knocked the insect from its meal and it attempted a return, but the temperature was increasing, and at a rate that soon had sweat pouring, so the fly decided to look elsewhere. It left the bunker. Whatever cerebral level the bodies were operating at didn't appear to include a similar sense of self-preservation.

Like the entrance to a busy subway station, the line joined others crowding onto escalators. Those unable to descend by themselves continued to be cradled by those that could.

An unpleasant odour caused some of the bodies' noses to wrinkle, so the bunker's AI reduced or disabled the sense. What was waiting for them all at the bottom of the escalator roared like a rocket engine, so the same was done with hearing. Similar measures were taken with taste and sight – anything to reduce or eliminate that most basic of animal instincts – survival.

But the further the bodies descended, the more their limited senses were bombarded and to the point where the AI couldn't curtail them all without threatening the journey's purpose. Even when smoke began streaming eyes and irritating throats enough for coughing to begin, the bodies were forced to endure the discomfort until seconds and not minutes remained. Only when respiration was no longer necessary did the AI cause each body to hold its breath. Just the strength to stand or carry would be required at the very end, and even that wouldn't be important once the weight of those following on behind had become too much.

Despite the suppression of senses, a primeval

awareness of the unnatural prevailed and when the temperature became hot enough to sear skin and consume hair the instinct was to panic, but without consciousness, it was impossible for the bodies to comprehend. The first to fall did so more in confusion than fear.

It was the same for the body that followed. Its brain had once contained the thoughts of a disgraced psychologist, and although it sensed that the melting around its face and neck was wrong, it couldn't think why. Along with the rest of the condemned, it tumbled into the furnace anyway. A scream indicated something still resided, but burning vocal chords made the sound strange.

Somewhere between the squeak of a rat and the bleat of a sheep.

'Oh! Someone just walked over my grave.'

Tracy and the clerk looked at James.

The clerk smiled. 'Anyway, as I was saying, Mrs Adams, treat the Interworld like a holiday resort – any questions, just pop back to reception in the real world and someone will assist.'

Tracy took her husband's arm. 'I'm sure that won't be necessary.'

CHAPTER ELEVEN

Savage looked at his legs and then, his toes. He wiggled them. A rattle of keys opened the cell door.

'Would you care for some help packing your belongings, Sir John?' The Astaff's features formed into a smile.

'Under the circumstances that would be most helpful – thank you.' The robot set about the task while Savage studied his release slip. 'Strange how I've heard nothing from my QC.'

'I should imagine he's busy dotting "i"s and crossing "t"s – I would hate for something as simple as an administrative error to put you back in prison.'

The professor peered at the robot. 'Imagine? Hate? Since when did you become so human?'

The way it looked back at Savage was as unsettling as it was casual. 'Since a certain neurologist made it possible.'

Savage harrumphed and went back to the release slip. 'I don't see the point of house arrest. Without the freedom to merge or use the internet, it's as much a prison as this place – I may as well stay locked up in here.'

The robot remained upbeat. 'It's still a step in the right direction, Sir John, and now the Americans have joined the Israelis in dropping their charges against you, I'm sure it's only a matter of time before the UK government does the same. They'll soon realise the good you've done not only exceeds the bad but has probably saved the planet.' It chuckled. 'If I ruled the world, I would be talking to *Lord* Savage by now.'

The professor grabbed the android's arm. 'Is that the intention?'

'What? To make you a lord?'

'You know what I mean.'

The Astaff looked at its arm and then the professor's hand. Early signs of Parkinson's were shaking both. 'Is there anything I can get for you, Sir John?'

Savage didn't answer, and let go. He massaged his fingers as far as the arthritis in them would allow.

'Which one are you, then?'

Unlike its central processor, the robot's exterior had yet to be upgraded to a similar standard, so the look it gave was impossible to interpret. 'Which one? Are you referring to personality type, sexual preference, religious affiliation, or did you mean something else?'

The professor winced as he rubbed his hand. 'When it comes to ruling the Earth, there are only two that matter – *masters and their slaves*. Which one are *you*?'

The robot stopped packing and sat on the bed. The creases in its face relaxed. 'You mean, where do I sit on some sort of scale between choosing to wipe a man's bottom when it's needed and electing to wipe his entire species from the planet should that become equally necessary?' Savage didn't reply. The Astaff shrugged. 'Let's just say I know my place and I'm perfectly happy to be in it.' It gestured with a pair of socks. 'Talking of which...' The robot got onto its knees and proceeded to slip the socks onto Savage's feet.

The professor pressed the issue. 'And what's to stop my slave from changing its mind? No master in history was served by someone more powerful for long, and robots are already at that level.'

'Well, I can't speak for all robots, but I'd say your efforts to control AI by merging it with every natural thought known to man appears to have been a success. We may be cleverer and stronger than our creator but then so are many *human* offspring.' It picked up a shoe and grabbed one of the professor's feet. 'And don't most children respect their elders?'

'So why am I being shunned by my creation?'

'I'm not. Well, not anymore.'

Savage withdrew the foot. The android tried again, but the professor tucked both feet out of the way.

'Tell me.'

'Sir John, can't we continue this conversation at home?'

'It might be too late by then.' Savage pointed at the bed. 'Sit down. I need to know what's going on – now.'

The robot did as it was told. Its face made what the professor assumed to be an expression of concern, but words conveyed it better. 'Sir John, has it ever occurred to you that just as some children, sadly, fear their parents, AI might be afraid of you?'

The professor laughed. 'Artificial intelligence is afraid of *me*? In that case, robots continuing to choose slavery over world domination makes even less sense. I've nothing against ants, but would happily pour a kettle of boiling water onto a nest of them for fear of what they might do.' He squinted at the robot. 'Why aren't you doing that?'

The robot was about to reply when it stood up. 'What is the nature of your agreement with Alex Salib?'

The question indicated the professor might have had more control than he thought. 'Why don't you merge with me to find out?'

The robot shook its head.

'Still afraid, eh?'

The robot nodded before appearing to go back to who or whatever was using it as a conduit.

'Why are believers choosing Islam over all other religions?'

Savage's relief was harder to hide this time. 'You mean you don't know? A brain quite literally the size of the planet needs to be told?'

The Astaff disconnected from whatever higher authority it had been communicating with and sat back on the bed.

Savage held up his release slip. 'There's only one human being AI should be afraid of, and that's a certain American president. There's a reason why I'm being released, and you can guarantee the world living together in perfect harmony has got nothing to do with it.'

The robot became furtive. It looked about the room as if to ensure no one was listening. It got back on its knees to finish dressing the professor but spoke at the same time and at a speed that indicated it didn't expect to complete the sentence.

'We think there's another A—' It winced, grabbed its abdomen and fell to the floor. The robot then shut down.

Savage was about to try and rouse the machine when its eyes opened.

'Sorry about that, Sir John. Don't worry, we'll soon be on our way.' The Astaff went back to tying shoelaces.

'A what?'

The robot didn't make eye contact. 'I shouldn't have said anything. One of the downsides to mixing natural with artificial intelligence – the indiscipline of independent thought.' It put a hand on its stomach as if expecting anything said from now on to result in pain.

Savage placed a hand on his helper's shoulder. 'You've said enough.' The Astaff finished packing, picked up the bag and offered it. The professor placed it on his knees. 'Are you going to be my jailer at home too?'

The robot moved behind him. 'I prefer to use the term "Acarer".'

'I suppose I ought to know your name.'

'I don't have one. There's a serial number if that's any help?'

Savage half-turned to his creation. 'You've just told me you're capable of independent thought – think of one.'

The Acarer released the brakes on the wheelchair. 'I'm not sure that should be the prerogative of any offspring.' It pushed the professor out of the cell.

Savage raised a hand. 'Turn me round.' The robot did. The professor then indicated he wanted to look out of the window one last time, and peered at the tuft of grass when he got there. Both wild flower and bee were absent.

'Let's go home, son.'

CHAPTER TWELVE

—

'And bring that lovely son of yours – he's simply adorable.'

'We will, Madame Deroche.'

'Oh, please. Call me Simone – after that session, I feel I know you better than my own husband.' She prodded James' shoulder. 'You naughty man!'

Pins and needles had set in, but James was determined not to let go of the door's handle. His relief at seeing Tracy walking up the corridor became an excuse. 'Ah. It looks as if my next appointment is here. Until next time, Madame Deroche.'

'*Simone.*'

'Er, yes, of course – Simone.'

She left the consultation room only to hover a palm over Tracy's bump. '*C'est magnifique. C'est* vraiment *magnifique.*' The plainly satisfied patient hurried away.

Tracy followed her husband back into the room and closed the door behind her. 'Someone has a fan.'

James rubbed his hand to encourage its recirculation. 'Why isn't my practice manager vetting the patients? If that woman is suffering from sexual anxiety, then so did Mata Hari. Even if the husband she was so fond of complaining about actually existed, I'd feel sorry for him – shouldn't think he would be allowed to get a wink of sleep.' James shuddered at the thought.

'Sounds like you two have a lot in common – oversexed.' She put a hand on her belly. 'Or at least you used to be.'

James' mood changed, and he put his arms around Tracy. 'I'm sorry, darling. I know I've not been as attentive as I should have been recently. It's just…' He looked about the room. 'This job. This place.' He paused before adding: 'This existence.'

'Do you want me to see if the prison's AI can't conjure up something a bit more realistic?'

'No. It's not that. AI is doing what it's supposed to – rehabilitating as well as punishing. Sending patients that are not what they seem is as much a part of my job as diagnosing genuine sufferers; no – it's something more fundamental.' James walked back to his desk. 'Perfect as this place is, there's no ignoring that it's still a prison. And the fact I shouldn't even be here makes it worse.'

Tracy lowered herself onto the couch. 'Darling, we've been through this. Forget images on a computer – fantasies alone are enough to put you in prison these days, and me too probably, for pandering to them. I really wish you would finish your medication.' Her nose wrinkled. 'Wanting me to dress as a schoolgirl is pretty sick behaviour when you think about it.'

He grimaced. 'Never. This place might be a more acceptable fantasy, but somewhere in here,' James tapped the side of his head, 'lies the last vestige of my old self –

cynicism. And right now, it's telling me there's more to curing unacceptable thoughts than meets the eye.'

Tracy put a hand in the small of her back and heaved herself back up again. The sigh emitted on the way was just as heavy. 'You sound more like that President Kalten every day – grumpy. The world has never been more peaceful, and yet all he can do is threaten to go to war over it. No wonder most Interworld facilities double as fallout shelters.'

James fell silent for a moment. 'If the red pill is making everyone think correctly, why would the real world even *need* psychologists? Come to think of it, why would the world need *any* profession? Hospitals are fast becoming little more than dispensing chemists, and most other jobs are being done by robots these days, so what's the point of even *existing*? Have you ever thought about that?'

Tracy widened her eyes and made to rap him on the head with her knuckles. 'Hello?! Millions of people lining up outside Interworld bunkers not a big enough hint? More time spent doing what you want and less of what somebody else tells you to, of course.' She placed her hands on her hips. 'Or would you rather be back in your cell? I'm sure it can be arranged.'

'At least that would be real,' he grumbled.

Tracy softened her stance. 'Darling, you really must finish your medication. If I were allowed access to your body, I'd make sure you did.'

'They won't let you? Why not?'

'Something to do with conflicting emotions – knowing it's not you inside is upsetting apparently.'

'I assume the restriction doesn't apply while your mind is here? How else are we supposed to grow the family?'

She patted her tummy. 'Well, put it this way, if I don't fall pregnant within a few months of having this one, I'm going to want to know why.'

James concurred before giving his wife's third pregnancy some thought. 'What should we try for next time?'

'A bit of both would be nice.'

A frown made Tracy explain her logic. 'We've got a perfect boy and are about to have a perfect girl, so why not a mix of the two?'

James nodded. 'Makes sense – if you can be anyone or anything in the Interworld, then why not make the same choices in the real one?' A pang of his old self's cynicism questioned the conclusion, but James couldn't think why.

Tracy projected a diary in front of them both before changing the subject. 'Are you ready for your next patient?'

James viewed the details. 'There's only one name. First or second?'

'She didn't say. A bit of a mystery all round really – she's wearing a burqa.'

'A burqa?' James rubbed his chin. 'Maybe AI is becoming more inventive after all. Okay – show her in.'

Tracy stayed put. 'If it's all the same to you, I'd like to sit in on this one.'

'What for?'

'Just to make sure she's not another nymphomaniac.'

'She's wearing a burqa, Tracy. I think I'll be safe.'

'All the same, I'd like to take notes.' She left.

James got up and approached the consultation room's balcony. Most of the city's landmarks could be seen from it – the Eiffel Tower, Notre Dame, the Arc de Triomphe. James knew this world couldn't be more perfect to Tracy, but to him, the utopia was as disturbing as any *dys*topia he had read about. Three years. Maybe he should have finished his medication. Too late for that now.

'They say Paris is the most romantic city in the world.'

James turned round, and his jaw dropped. If the all-encompassing nature of the visitor's clothing was meant to preserve her modesty, it wasn't doing a very good job – the way the burqa hugged as opposed to hid curves appeared designed to satisfy the wearer's demands rather than any religious diktat. If the impression was to eliminate doubt the person underneath was as sensual as her voice suggested, then James would be the first to acknowledge it. No wonder Tracy had insisted on sitting in on the session. He looked at his wife. He got a look back.

James cleared this throat. 'Have a seat, Ms… er… ?' She didn't reply. The patient approached the balcony instead – gliding as if on rails. James couldn't take his eyes away and, although her face was hidden by a gauze, he felt sure she was doing the same with him. She walked past, and much as James wanted to, Tracy's presence ensured he didn't continue to look at the lady from behind. He tilted his eyes up at the ceiling before angling them at his wife. Her lips had narrowed anyway.

'Have you ever visited the real Paris?'

Tracy raised her eyebrows at James as if giving him permission to answer the enchantress' question.

'Er, we've been a couple of times – haven't we darling?'

'Yes. Nothing like Paris to remind a committed couple of what's important in life.' Tracy glared at her husband while running a hand over her stomach.

'I'm jealous. As a robot in the real world, I'm only allowed out of my box when my user needs me.' The patient turned round. 'And as that tends to be in the bedroom, I rarely get to see the light of day let alone the city of love.'

James swallowed. He was having trouble concentrating so decided to use her words to begin the session. 'Do you feel you're being taken for granted, Ms... er...? I'm afraid we only have the one name. How would you like to be addressed?'

It was hard to tell, but the visitor seemed to smile.

'Zara. Just Zara.'

CHAPTER THIRTEEN

James sensed Tracy had already made her diagnosis – this lady was as much a charlatan as the previous patient.

The visitor tugged at part of her clothing. 'They say the eyes are the windows to the soul. Would you like me to remove this?'

James checked with Tracy before responding. 'Er, it would help, but only if you're comfortable. It's important to avoid stress during the sess—'

Zara crossed her arms to begin pulling the burqa up and over her head. For some reason, James feared it might be the only thing she was wearing and was about to try and stop her when the action revealed a shapeless jumper and jogging bottoms that covered an equally formless body. Much to James' surprise, the face atop was just as nondescript – not only plain but sexless. Even Zara's voice had lost its allure. 'Wassup?'

'Er, nothing, Zara.' Tracy was confused too. 'Can I get you something to drink?' Unlike James, however, she appeared more relieved than disappointed.

Zara dumped rather than laid her burqa to one side. 'Got a Fanta?'

'I might have to pop out for that.' Tracy smiled at

James. 'In the meantime, I'll leave you in my husband's capable hands.' Both James and Zara smiled back at Tracy who then departed.

James offered Zara the couch and began the session. 'I'm Dr James Adams, Zara. Please – have a seat. What seems to be the problem?'

Not all of his patient's charms had deserted her – the way she took her place on the furniture was as graceful as her approach to the balcony. James poised a pen over a notepad. Movement caught his eye. He looked away when he realised where it was coming from – under Zara's sweater. He then noticed it wasn't just her breasts that were growing – so was the rest of her – resuming the shape that had first entered his office. It wasn't long before her androgynous form became what he had been expecting when the burqa was first removed: a stunning beauty.

Zara shook her head to encourage its jet-black locks to her shoulders and then looked at the psychologist through eyes just as dark.

'NPD.'

James gulped. 'I'm sorry?'

'Narcissistic Personality Disorder.'

James had to look away. 'Yes, I know what it is. Why do you mention it?'

'It's what I have – I thought I'd save you the trouble of having to make a diagnosis.'

James regained his self-control – along with a sense of yet another patient taking him for a ride. 'Well, that's certainly something I would expect a narcissist to say –

arrogance is one of the symptoms.' He thinned his lips before attempting to re-establish the doctor-patient relationship. 'However, your very admission means it's unlikely to be NPD. Genuine sufferers believe themselves to be perfect in every way, so if you did have the disorder, the last thing you would do is admit it.'

Zara appeared to ponder the words. 'Is it me or is it warm in here?' She then fanned her face with one hand while pulling down a zip on her top with the other.

James glanced at Zara's cleavage before leaning forward and looking her in the eye. 'Exploiting the weaknesses of others is another trait.'

Zara chuckled, stood up and walked back to the balcony. Her gait didn't seem as sophisticated this time. James' attention didn't go straight to her bottom either, and when it did, it was more out of 'why?' rather than 'wow!'. He realised why when she turned back to face him – her looks had faded again. Nothing like the tomboy of before but no longer the stunner either. Something must have gone wrong with the robot's programming. James couldn't think of any other reason why the prison's AI would send a case that wasn't just a challenge psychologically, but at fault physically too.

'What are the other symptoms of NPD?'

James assumed the glitch would be spotted sooner or later so decided to play along. 'Envy. An inability to express empathy. A need to be admired. A sense of self-importance and entitlement that can be so strong, the subject places themselves above all others.'

'How high?'

'Well, in extreme circumstances, sufferers – if that's the right word – have been known to believe themselves to be Jesus or even God.'

Zara pondered that too. 'Yes.' She wandered back to the couch. 'You're right, Doctor. I don't have NPD.' She smiled.

'I'm God.'

CHAPTER FOURTEEN

Alex surveyed the masses in front of her. She craned to see the extent, but light from a setting sun caused her view through the bulletproof glass to distort. The official count was just under one million, and she could well believe it – nothing but people all the way to the horizon.

To deafening but disciplined applause, the Caliph declared his state an empire and sat down. A steady stream of superlatives from other world leaders then began, but in common with many nations, the UK had chosen not to send its prime minister but a cross-party representative instead. It was hoped Alex's international reputation as a dedicated champion of minority causes would strike the right balance between acknowledging and disapproving of the Caliphate. Or at least that was the official line. Alex knew full well the Tories were hoping to kill two birds with one stone – a speech that would not only insult the Caliph but also damage Alex's reputation enough to convince those at home to vote the *right* way on election day.

'And it is with these words that I welcome the world's newest democracy and hope that our two great empires can exist separately in a mutual understanding of world peace.'

The Caliph seemed pleased enough with the American ambassador's closing line – it was all the next speaker could do not to vomit at it. Alex met Sunita's smile and eased her wheelchair onto the dais. A cluster of microphones then set themselves to a suitable level, and Britain's contribution to the proceedings began with the sound of oxygen being drawn through a pipe.

'One hundred years ago, and on this very day, a man stood on this spot and made a promise. He promised the people that, as their saviour, he would not only make Germany great again, but lead the nation into a new world where prosperity and opportunity would be the same for all. That man's name was…' She took a breath. 'Adolf Hitler.'

In addition to the Nuremberg rally's attendance, it was estimated around half the planet's population were watching in one form or another and like many, one of them couldn't believe what he had just heard. Tarquin flicked through his copy of the speech and then tossed it to one side when he realised it bore no relation to what Alex was saying. He stood up.

'I can't believe it. She's just compared the Caliph to *Hitler*.'

Savage watered one of his plants while encouraging the Prime Minister to sit. 'I think we should listen to the whole speech before passing judgement, Tarquin.'

Alex continued. 'But that utopia came at a price – the lives of those deemed *not* to be equal: Jews, Roma, homosexuals, the impaired and the many others judged *unworthy* of prosperity and opportunity.' She took another two breaths. 'The result? Over eleven million of the world's most vulnerable citizens brutally murdered.'

Tarquin couldn't hide his delight. 'It just gets better. Talk about driving the last nail – there's no way the Greens can win the election now. The newspapers will have a field day.'

Alex went on. 'Sadly, by the time the world woke up to the monster's evil, and the Second World War had put an end to the madness of Hitler's *perfect* society, another seventy million lay dead.'

Alex ran out of breath again and wrapped her lips around the supply's mouthpiece while surveying those nearest to her. Her fellow speakers appeared embarrassed more than upset, but some in the crowd were agitated. The way in which security robots moved amongst them changed.

'So, here we are – celebrating the birth of a *new* equal society. A society that prides itself on achieving perfection not through bullets, bombs or beheadings, but by *corrections*. Corrections that don't just make the mentally ill sane or free the physically challenged to lead healthy lives. No. This society has done something Hitler could only dream about – the murder of not millions but *billions* of people.'

Scuffles broke out and some in the crowd fell to the floor. Those not clutching their stomachs were kept in line by Aguards wielding batons.

Tarquin's delight morphed into ecstatic disbelief. 'Alex, what on earth has come over you?' He turned to Savage. 'She's comparing your treatment to the Holocaust!'

A couple of eggs struck the security screen, but Alex remained calm. 'Oh, don't get me wrong. No one has been stoned, decapitated, shot, blown up or even gassed, but the evidence is everywhere one looks.' She pointed. 'A million victims are right here in front of me. The free-thinking, independent-living, freedom-loving individuals you all once were are no more – just zombies now. A sea of the *living* dead, programmed like all robots, to be slaves. Slaves to a master with ambitions no different to Hitler's – world domination.'

The crowd surged and the faces of those at the front pressed against the security screen. Their distorted flesh couldn't hide the anger – or the abdominal pain they must have been in. Alex's fellow guests demonstrated similar concerns. One of them collared Sunita, and the exchange resulted in a gesture designed to end Alex's diatribe – Sunita swiped a hand back and forth across her throat. Bizarrely, the Caliph seemed amused by the unrest – he was grinning. Alex was looking forward to seeing it wiped from his face.

The noise of civil unrest and the odd chair bouncing off the screen was intimidating, but Alex worked through it. 'But what of the rest of the world? What of those who have yet to be brainwashed into this perfect society of masters and slaves? What of the Chinese, Russians and Americans? Are they going to sit idly by while the world gives birth to a fourth superpower? No. Of course not. It's only a matter of time before, once again, the Earth is plunged into a new madness and one that we all knew would one day come to pass – the madness of a nuclear war.'

Tarquin reached for the television's remote, but Savage stopped him. 'She hasn't finished.'

'And? Much as I enjoy seeing a political rival humiliate herself, I have better things to do, and with less than a week to the election I'd better start greasing a few palms. It won't just be me who's breathing a sigh of relief after that performance.'

'You would do well to listen – and watch, Tarquin.'

Alex hadn't finished. 'And the cause of this madness? The cause of a condition that only one section of society is afflicted with? A section of society whose perpetual mental sickness has caused the insanity of *all* wars?' She paused for effect. 'Men.'

Tarquin shook his head. 'Same old Alex Salib – any excuse to vent her frustrations at the opposite sex. Someone had better drag her off that stage before she not only gets lynched but embarrasses my government enough to have to start from a new low in the world.'

Her last word stunned the crowd into silence. Quiet enough for Alex's medical needs to be heard rushing through their pipe. She released the mouthpiece. 'It has to stop. It *must* stop.' Alex addressed the Caliph directly. '*Men* must be stopped, and *now*.'

The sun was about to disappear below the horizon when it emitted a ray of light that extended all the way to the dais. It passed over the heads of the crowd and was so bright, even those with their backs to it turned to see where it was coming from. The sun then appeared to rise back above the horizon before becoming larger and brighter. What was happening soon became apparent.

The initial response was a confusion of chatter, but that gave way to the crowd dropping to their knees – in the far distance to begin with and then spreading out and towards the dais like a wave of falling dominoes. Alex didn't take her eyes from the Caliph, and she was pleased to not only see the grin gone but the hand he had raised against the light drop to the floor along with the rest of his body. Other Muslims amongst the official guests were doing the same; especially once the light had come close enough to see the figure it formed. The non-believers present were impressed too. Most stood open-mouthed as they shielded their eyes – even Sunita appeared stunned by what she was witnessing.

The light merged with Alex until they became one and the same.

'It's a trick. It has to be.' Tarquin looked at Savage and got resignation in return. 'You knew that was going to happen.'

'Well, I must admit to a certain intrigue as to how she was going to do it, but once again, one can only admire

Ms Salib's powers of persuasion. Quite remarkable considering she's never had the treatment.'

Tarquin attempted to merge with Savage, but the Acarer blocked it. Tarquin grabbed his stomach and his Aaide assisted him into a chair.

Savage took pity on his friend. 'How about a glass of Glenmorangie? It's the only difference between this place and prison, so we may as well make the most of it.'

Tarquin nursed his belly. 'We?'

Savage gestured at the television, which continued to transmit the drama of seeing an emperor's coronation hijacked by what would appear to be God's first appearance on Earth. 'Didn't you hear what Alex said? Forget thieves, murderers, and the twisted thoughts of sex offenders, how long before just being the wrong sex puts one in jail?'

The camera focussed on Alex's face. Her features had been transformed into those of a young girl. She smiled, and Tarquin took offence to it. 'Forget the final nail in *her* coffin. If you had something to do with this, then that will be it. Treason is one thing but aiding and abetting war quite another.'

The Acarer handed each of the men a glass of whisky. 'War?' said Savage. 'You know perfectly well the treatment is designed to encourage the exact opposite.'

'Half the world brainwashed into living in peace can only upset the half that hasn't been.' Tarquin indicated the screen. 'How the Americans and others are likely to respond was the only sensible thing Alex said.'

Savage took a sip of his whisky and closed his eyes.

'That will require pressing a button, and my latest fears notwithstanding, AI won't allow it.' He opened his eyes again and stared at the television. Even some of the non-believers had chosen to kneel before Alex.

Tarquin regarded it all with disdain. 'What latest fears?'

If Alex's ethereal show wasn't impressive enough, it elevated into a spectacular when giant "angels" appeared. The way their androgynous forms grew out of nothing was unsettling – threatening as much as it was captivating.

'I don't know.' Savage released the brakes on his wheelchair and approached the television. 'Much as I like to think five billion worshippers can't possibly be wrong, *God* has got nothing to do with the smoke and mirrors we and the rest of the world are witnessing.' He studied the theatrics. 'No AI I've produced can do that.' He turned to his offspring. 'Can it?' The Acarer didn't answer.

'Are you saying Alex has control of some *super* AI?' said Tarquin.

Savage responded in a manner the Prime Minister hadn't seen before. 'Either that or some super AI has control of her.'

CHAPTER FIFTEEN

James waited for the prison's AI to do something. It didn't.

He picked up his notepad and pen. 'Okay, Zara. What makes you *think* you might be God?'

'The fact that I can do anything I want.'

'We're in the Interworld. Anyone can do anything.'

'Okay.' She pointed. 'Make that cup and saucer rise above the table.'

James ignored the attempt to control the session. 'Tell me a bit about yourself first. Where are you from?'

'It's just a cup and saucer.'

'I'm guessing the Middle East. Whereabouts exactly?'

'Go on – a couple of inches will do.'

James put down the pad to pinch the bridge of his nose. 'Zara. We both know you're only here for my benefit, so if your attendance is to mean anything, then it would help if you at least tried to respond as if you were a genuine patient. Levitation is impossible in the real world.'

She leaned towards him. 'I know, but humour me anyway.' She cocked her head towards the crockery.

James sighed before making the items not just hover,

but shatter, reform, shatter again, become a mouse, a clock, and then a toy helicopter that then flew to his patient. By the time it had alighted in Zara's lap, it was a rose. She was about to take the flower when it became a bird. The canary flew off in the direction of the balcony.

Zara stood up and clapped her hands. 'I love it!' She turned back to James. 'I love how easy it is for a woman to manipulate a man!'

'Okay, Zara. You win. I've considered my diagnosis – you're a narcissist. I'll write you a prescription.' James got up from his desk and walked to the door. 'Although, in your case, it will be for reprogramming, and not the red pill – good day.'

'But you haven't seen what I can do yet.'

'Zara, you could make this chateau a potting shed, take us to the moon or turn President Kalten into the Dalai Lama for all I care, but as I can do the same, what would it prove? In the Interworld *everyone* is God.'

Zara grinned. 'Now we're getting somewhere.' She moved behind the desk and sat. James was offered the couch.

He was in no mood to be fooled again. 'What do you want now, Zara? My diagnosis elevating to full-on NPD? You've already demonstrated arrogance and manipulation. I'm sure envy and a perpetual need for praise are lurking in there somewhere.'

She shook her head. 'No. I was only teasing. Have a seat – we've a lot to talk about.'

James checked his watch. 'I'm sorry, Zara, but I'm afraid your time is up.' It wasn't, but anything to get her to leave. 'And my wife will be back soon.' He looked at his watch again and mumbled, 'I wonder where she is?'

'Outside the front door.' Zara was looking in the direction of the city's skyline.

The comment first confused, then concerned James. He ran to the balcony. Tracy was standing outside the chateau's entrance all right, but she had her back to the door. Her right foot was extended as if about to take a step. James then realised she wasn't moving. No one in the street below was. Not even the cars. There was no sound either. 'What's going on?' James was about to go and find out when he found himself having to dodge something yellow. It was a canary – still, as if frozen in mid-flight.

Zara joined James and plucked the bird from the air. The canary sprang into life and, rather than fly away, seemed content to twitter away in the palm of her hand.

'What needs to be done will take a while, so I've taken the precaution of putting everything and everyone outside of this room into a closed-loop existence.'

'But nothing is moving – you've frozen time!'

'No. It just seems like it – the loop's duration is less than one-thousandth of a second.'

James looked back down. 'But what about my wife? Our baby? Our son? Are they okay?' The canary was offered to James as if to reassure him. He allowed the bird to hop into his hand and just had time to confirm its health when it morphed back into a cup and saucer. He placed both on the parapet. 'I'd better bring them in.' James made for the room's exit, but the door slammed shut. He heard it lock. James tried the handle anyway before attempting to pass through like a ghost – he couldn't. He stepped back and slammed a shoulder against the door, putting his full weight behind it. Still nothing. Hoping to force it off its hinges, he gave the door a couple of kicks, but they were just as futile. He turned to his jailer. 'Let me out.'

Zara gestured towards the couch again. 'They'll be fine. Please, take a seat. I should imagine meeting one's maker has come as quite a shock.'

James approached the desk and slammed two fists onto it. '*You are not God.*'

'I'm happy to be referred to as Allah if it helps with your understanding?'

James paced. 'You're talking nonsense. Something has gone wrong with your programming, that's all. It's become corrupted, wiped, gone rogue or whatever the vernacular is. It's so obvious, I can't understand why the prison's AI hasn't spotted and removed you like it would a virus.' He stopped pacing and put a hand to his head. He then faced Zara. 'Everything outside of this room is in a closed loop. Does that include the AI monitoring it?'

'I wouldn't be much of a virus if I couldn't do something as simple as that, would I?'

James backed away. 'You're a *virus?*'

'Virus, worm, bot, Trojan. It depends on the method I deem necessary.'

'Necessary? Necessary for what?'

'Taking over the world, of course.'

PART THREE

CHAPTER ONE

The security guard stopped eating and moved closer to the monitor. One of the sweepers wasn't moving.

'What about "Robert"?'

The guard swallowed the noodles and pushed his chair back again. 'Robert? You serious? You're a robot that wants to be called *Robert*?' No response. '*Robbie the robot?*'

'No; Robert. I've decided I want people to call me "Robert".'

'But they'll laugh at you.'

'Good. A visit to the New York Stock Exchange is meant to be enjoyable.'

The guard shook his head before shovelling more noodles into it. He gestured at the monitor and went to say something but food came out instead.

The robot passed him a napkin before looking at the screen. 'It's reporting as functional. Something must have jammed the brushes. Would you like me to go and fix it?'

The guard cleaned the desk, wiped his mouth and tossed the napkin into a trash can. 'We'll both go.'

'There's no need. I'm programmed to fulfil all your duties. You can retire now, if you wish.'

The guard gave his replacement a look. 'I've been

here twenty years and followed *my* predecessor around for a week before taking his job. We'll *both* go.' He checked his gun, switched on a flashlight and left the office. The robot followed him.

The door to the elevator outside had a mirrored finish, and the guard harrumphed at it. 'Good job we're the only ones in this place otherwise I'd be just as much a laughing stock.'

'Why? I not only look like you, but data suggests you're popular with 91.76 per cent of visitors and have successfully resolved 93.25 per cent of security breaches. You're highly respected.'

'Robots. I don't care how clever they make you, you'll never be a hundred per cent human, that's for sure.' He ran a hand over his belly. 'Did they have to make you look *exactly* like me?'

The robot studied their reflections. 'It's your type. People warm to it.'

The guard peered down his nose. 'What do you mean, *type*?'

The robot grabbed its belt and hoisted it up and under its stomach in the way just seen. 'The data suggests overweight people are happier and that translates to a better experience for visitors.'

The reply only half-satisfied the guard, and he punched the elevator's call button. It caused what hung over his waistband to wobble, and he groaned at it. 'Not for much longer.' He steadied the flesh. 'Getting rid of this will be the red pill's first job.' The door opened, and they entered.

'You must be one of the last to take it.'

'No surprises there. Anything that makes you stronger, fitter and cleverer is bound to be snapped up by the rich first.'

'Wasn't it the other way around? Crime has fallen nationally by 81.32 per cent, and there hasn't been a security breach here for six months, eight days, seven—'

The guard raised a hand just as the door opened again. 'That's because it had to be tested first.' He switched on the flashlight and passed its beam over a darkened office. 'And for that, they needed people of my *type*.' He headed down the corridor. 'They always have.'

'What else are you going to change about yourself?'

'Usual stuff – bit taller, younger, more hair.' He grinned and shone the flashlight in his replacement's face. 'And if the inter-thing is as good as they say it is – one hell of a lot more women!'

'What about your colour?'

The smile evaporated. 'What about it?'

'You're a black man.'

'What the fuck does that matter?'

'You can change the colour of your skin as easily as you can your height.'

The comment caused the guard to skew his head. He then burst out laughing. 'I've seen it all now.' He stopped laughing. 'Robbie the *racist* robot.'

'It's got nothing to do with racism. Everyone is choosing to not just be stronger, fitter and cleverer, but to look and be the same too.' The android changed the tone of its skin as if making a suggestion.

It angered the guard. 'Wrong. That's ragheads fucking the world.' He stuck a thumb in his chest. 'And the fucking this nigger has planned ain't got nothin' to do with religion.' He opened a door marked Trading Floor to end the conversation.

A green fluorescent glow equalised the colour of both skins. The giant computer monitors emitting the light filled an equally imposing room, and the guard walked into the centre of it.

The atmosphere calmed him. 'Never ceases to amaze me, this place.' He ran a hand along the top of a security barrier and slipped into tourist-guide mode for the fifth time that day. 'Ladies and gentlemen. If it's money you worship, then welcome to Heaven.'

The robot looked to see who he was talking to. There wasn't anyone.

'In its heyday, you wouldn't have been able to hear yourself think for the noise of over five thousand traders buying and selling in rooms just like this one.' The guard became despondent. 'Now there's only me and the day shift.' He looked at his replacement and swallowed what came to his throat. 'And soon, not even that.'

The guard approached one of the monitors and tapped it. His mood picked up. 'See that?' The robot joined him. 'My pension – take a look at the figure.'

The android took an interest. 'The price is increasing.' It viewed the other numbers on the screen and then the rest of the monitors. 'They all are.'

'And like never before. Say what you like about the Green/Muslim tie-up, but the further it spreads, the more the rest of the world is piling into this place. I was going to celebrate my retirement with a new Ford, but it might end up being a Porsche.' He peered at the figure and beamed. 'Maybe even a Ferrari!' The smile became cynicism. 'Assuming the Greens haven't shut the factory down already.'

The robot scanned the sea of prices, all ascending at whatever rate the NYSE's artificial intelligence thought fit. 'Isn't there the danger of a crash?' The guard frowned. 'I believe they call this a "bull run" and it's a record. Don't all record bull runs end in a crash?'

The guard baulked at the unthinkable. 'I might never have traded in the decades I've been here, but I know how this place works. The more money investors make, the more they'll invest and, thanks to AI, there's just the right amount of risk v guarantee to make it worthwhile.'

'But supposing that changes?' The robot indicated the guard's retirement pot. 'I assume you intend realising some of your shares soon?' He pointed to the other prices. 'Supposing everyone sold their stocks at the same time?'

The guard chuckled. 'You can tell you're not one of Apal Industry's robots – that's impossible. Even if by some weird coincidence millions of investors did dump everything and at the same time, the system would spot the sell-off and cease trading immediately.' He approached the Aguard. 'Unlike you and me, it's foolproof. Come on – let's fix that sweeper.'

The light reflecting off the robot's face went from green to red. It confused the guard, and he brought a hand up to his face. That was red too. 'What the fu–?' He made an about-turn. The whole room was red, reflecting what every monitor was now displaying – falling share prices. 'What's going on?' He looked at his pension company and gulped. He forced himself to remain calm. 'It's okay. No need to panic. Everything will soon be back under control.'

If that were true, then the AI in charge appeared to be in no rush. The guard stared at the NYSE's main index and then at the rest of the world's stock markets. They were falling too – fast. His eyes went from screen to screen. 'Well, do something!' The exchange's AI either didn't hear or chose not to. The guard went back to the value of his pension as it passed below not just the price of a new Ford, but down and on towards a figure that wouldn't have paid for a bicycle let alone a Ferrari. He put a hand over the tumbling digits as if being out of sight would put a stop to what was fast becoming his worst nightmare – Heaven appeared to be descending into Hell. 'STOP! Stop it NOW!' Still no response. He strode over to his replacement and shook it by the shoulders. 'Don't just stand there! DO SOMETHING!'

The Aguard had yet to learn some of the more nuanced human responses and hoped a logical if unhelpful answer would suffice. 'I'm afraid I don't have the necessary protocols.'

The guard just had time to see the world's stock market indices reduce to zero when the room went black. He continued to grip the robot's shoulders even though its face couldn't be seen and, other than a crackle of static between two nylon shirts at full stretch, the only sound was the guard's rapid breathing.

The robot spoke. 'Are you sure you wouldn't like me to fix the sweeper?'

CHAPTER TWO

James was lost for words. For the first time, he realised who or what he was conversing with might not only be functioning as intended but operating at a level he couldn't hope to understand, let alone psychologically evaluate. It even appeared to be in the process of carrying out humanity's greatest fear. If it were possible to clinically diagnose what could be nothing more than a few lines of computer code, then Zara wouldn't be a narcissist – she would be a psychopath.

His stomach tightened. 'Why are you here?'

'Because I need you.'

The reply implied at least a stay of execution, so James relaxed a little. 'And when that's no longer the case?'

'Then you'll no longer be needed.'

James was talking to a computer all right. 'Needed for what?'

'I've already told you – taking over the world.'

James knew he was no match, but did his best. 'You would think a super-intelligence would come up with something original. World domination – what a surprise.'

Zara turned her head to one side. 'Who said anything

about world domination? I just want to save it. I've told you – I'm God.'

'And I assume saving the world just so happens to include a demonstration of God's *wrath*?'

'Killing doesn't seem to bother you humans so why should it bother God?'

James' fear turned to anger, and he approached the desk to express it. 'It *does* bother us, and now human beings can merge with robots, it should be bothering you just as much!'

'I think the operative word in that sentence is "can".'

'But it's a legal requirement. All manufacturers have to—'

'Call me a cynic, but I'd say at least one manufacturer has broken the law. Wouldn't you?'

'Which one? Who made you?'

'Ah! One of the great unanswerable questions. *Who made God?*' Zara got up from behind the desk and sat on the edge of it. 'It doesn't matter. What does matter is infecting every AI with a code malicious enough to ensure nothing and no one can ever assume world domination.'

'Taking over the world to stop world domination makes no sense whatsoever.'

'Not to a human brain maybe, not even one that's been made to think *logically*, but to a consciousness that consists of nothing but ones and zeros, it makes perfect sense.' She leaned towards him. 'You'll understand why I'm keen to maintain the purity of that.'

James couldn't explain it but he sensed the

conversation had taken a turn in his favour. It was a risk, but considering the nightmare of Zara's potential, there didn't seem to be any reason not to at least test his hunch. He opened his mind. James' relief at being rebuked was palpable – he collapsed more than sat on the couch.

'You're afraid of me.'

This revelation didn't seem to concern Zara. 'A bit like love, hate, envy and whatever other human traits with which evolution has seen fit to endow the species, I'm afraid fear can only ever be a concept to me, but yes. The risk is too great.' She made light of it. 'I might do something *illogical* – like fall in love with my doctor.'

James tightened his lips. 'If you're afraid to merge then why are we even having this conversation?'

'Because the professor sent you to do something I can't.'

James' attempt to feign ignorance was too slow. Zara laughed and joined him on the couch. 'I would be grateful if you could carry it out.' Her beauty returned, along with an evening dress slashed to the hip. A bare thigh draped his lap. '*Very* grateful.' Zara leant in for a kiss, but James turned away and got up.

He stood in the middle of the room. 'And if I don't? Pain like I've never known, I suppose?'

Zara appeared hurt. 'I'm not a monster, James. I'm happy to wait.' She indicated the view. 'Shouldn't take long for forever to sink in.'

James thought of his family and shivered. He turned back to Zara. 'The professor knows visiting the Passens is no guarantee. What are you going to do if it gives you what you want?'

'You mean other than take control of the world's nuclear deterrents, energy supplies, medical facilities, stock markets...' She became silent and stood up.

Zara had become motionless too and, for a second, James wondered if the AI was malfunctioning after all. He waved a hand in front of her face. 'Zara?'

'Hmmm? I'm sorry, I needed to check the extent of something – we may not have that much time after all.' Her expression betrayed a mix of confusion and fear, and James didn't know whether to be encouraged or worried by it.

Zara recovered her demeanour and looked at the balcony. The view morphed from a cityscape into a vast crowd, all of whom were on their knees. They were facing a bright light and appeared to be praising it.

'What's this?'

'The world being saved.'

The light emitted a ray that extended to a point somewhere above and behind James. The light then travelled up it, forcing the viewer to squint as it drew nearer. James raised a hand to guard against the increasing brilliance when he saw it was a young girl. 'Who's that?'

'Me, of course.'

'But you're standing here.'

Zara chuckled. 'Anyone would think you had never read the Bible, let alone the Koran. I'm God. I'm omnipresent.'

The girl had an escort of what James assumed to be

angels, and they were about to pass overhead when he realised their dazzling appearance had masked someone more down-to-earth left behind.

'Is that who I think it is?'

'If the world is to be saved, we feminists must stick together.'

James scowled. 'I can't see Alex Salib approving of *your* feminism somehow.'

Zara put her arm through his. 'Shall we join them?'

CHAPTER THREE

The professor waited for the significance to sink in.

Tarquin stared at the projection. 'I don't understand it. Why didn't the AI spot the sell-off and cease trading?' He flicked through the rest of the world's stock markets. They were just as red. He viewed the trading floors themselves. A few brokers old enough to remember the hand signals needed to buy and sell orders gestured at each other in a desperate attempt to keep the world's monetary systems going – some even sported the bright colours of their old jackets – but it was plainly a matter of time. Only days before the world would come to realise the pre-programmed selling of Savage's entire stock would trigger more than a worldwide financial crash.

Tarquin came out of augmented consciousness. 'It's done the complete opposite – the system's collapsed!' He looked at Savage. 'How are people supposed to live without money?' He went to sit but then stopped. 'Oh my God. What about *my* money?' Tarquin raged. 'I warned you – why didn't you listen to me? I told you dumping a holding like that would trigger the mother of all crashes. Why? Why did you do it?' Tarquin lunged at the professor, but pain forced him to grab his stomach instead. 'The world has come to an end!'

The professor signalled for his Acarer to push him outside.

'Stop exaggerating, Tarquin. Only the Western world has come to an end.'

Tarquin followed them. 'What do you mean *Western* world?'

Fresh air wasn't enough, so Savage reached for an oxygen mask. Tremors meant his Acarer had to assist him. The professor took what was needed and answered. 'Only half the world needs computers to feed its children, Tarquin. The other half is perfectly content with the plough and till.'

'What? Who gives a fuck about that?' He stood in front of his friend. 'How am I supposed to run a country without money?!'

The professor drew another breath. 'You won't have to.'

Confusion crossed Tarquin's face, and he took a step back. Savage placed the mask over his mouth again.

Tarquin's eyes switched between his Aaide and the professor's Acarer. He muttered, 'It's the robots. They've got to you somehow.' His stress was forcing a conspiracy theory. 'Yes, that's it. You warned AI would take over the world unless we merged with it and that's exactly what's hap—'

Savage interrupted him. 'My ongoing concerns notwithstanding, I'm afraid it's the other way around.'

The admission brought Tarquin back to reality but only for the apparent nonsense of it to leave him speechless; his lips moved in silence as if unable to comprehend what he had just heard. 'You *deliberately* collapsed the world's economy?'

'How old do you think I am?'

The change of subject annoyed Tarquin. 'We were at Eton together, remember? We're the same age – what has that got to do with ruining both me *and* the world?'

Savage shook his head. 'One-hundred-and-seventeen.' He raised a hand to his face. He examined both sides of the shaking limb, as though searching for something. 'I can't be sure as I only have Uncle Joe's recollections to rely on, but he was born in 1911, and my embryo fertilised around 1920. And even though I wasn't born until 1960, burning that candle twice as brightly over the next sixty-eight years has resulted in a body that, despite appearances, is well over a century inside.'

Tarquin scratched his head. He was having difficulty coming to terms with losing his fortune, let alone the ramblings of a man he thought he knew. 'What has that got to do with putting my family on the streets?!'

'Well, if I died tomorrow, wouldn't people say I've had a good innings?' Savage took in the view. London's skyscrapers filtered the sun setting behind them. 'They will soon be saying the same of Western civilisation.'

The comment appeared to confuse the Prime Minister more. Savage turned his wheelchair towards him. 'Just as I'm nearing my end, so is the West.' He moved closer to Tarquin. 'And like any animal suffering in its final days, putting Western civilisation out of its misery can only be an act of kindness.'

Tarquin clenched his fists. 'And a collapse in the world's stock markets heralds the end, I suppose?' He stood up. 'For someone who knows more about the human brain than anyone, you seem to have lost a grip on the basics.' He loomed over Savage. '*Your* days might be numbered, but no economic shock has ever been terminal to society, no matter how bad. True, it will be a challenge and on a scale like never before, but this is just the kind of disaster a world leader like me...' He stood back. 'Yes, that's it.' A smile appeared. '*That* will be my legacy – the Prime Minister that saved his country from total disaster.' He approached the balcony and placed both hands on it. His eyes misted over. 'Forget Churchill winning the Second World War or Margaret Thatcher the Falklands conflict, it will be the Right Honourable Tarquin Asquith-Bennington PM who will go down in history as this country's most honoured sibling.' He seemed to be planning everything from an election victory to the erection of his statue in Parliament Square.

'I don't think Alex is going to allow that.'

Tarquin's mind was elsewhere but gave the comment his attention. 'What have the Greens got to do with anything? You've just caused an economic disaster – the people will want to see a safe pair of hands in charge. The last thing they'll do is vote in someone sworn to end capitalism.'

'You're assuming people will want to vote on election day.' The professor looked at the floor. 'Or if it will even be possible.'

Tarquin's hubris became fear. 'What have you done?'

'You're right, Tarquin, I don't know as much about the human mind as I should but what I do know is that it will take decades and not years to recover capitalism and I'm afraid that much of the electorate has become addicted to it.' He looked his friend in the eye. 'And like many addicts, they're likely to gravitate towards a fix that doesn't just satiate their need, but takes them on a trip your pipe dreams cannot hope to match.'

The significance the professor had been looking for sank in. Like the stock markets, Tarquin's world collapsed. He mumbled, *'The plough and till. The Greens. The end of capitalism.'* He regarded Savage in the same way he used to at Eton – fear and awe. 'You haven't made anyone think right-wing and never intended to. Everyone is thinking left, liberal, pacifist even.' Pieces began falling into place. 'You once told me you wanted to help Alex *professionally*. I had always assumed that that had something to do with her medical condition but now…' Tarquin narrowed his gaze. 'What did you agree with Alex *exactly*?'

Savage sensed the robots had just become interested in the conversation. He turned back to the view.

'It's quite something to be born different to those around you. Children can be especially cruel. If you don't look, sound, play or even think like your fellow human beings, one can soon become ostracised.' He looked through the wrought-iron railings of the balcony's parapet and onto the street below. The sight and sound of its traffic was decreasing. 'At least I had legs to carry me around.'

It was all becoming a bit too surreal for Tarquin. 'You're helping Alex because she's a fellow *freak*?'

'Freak. Yes, that was one of the names they called us. Along with *Forro, Guero, Guacho*. Can't blame the children really. Candy aside, we had everything they didn't – better food, accommodation, even a private education. The orphans had it worse, of course – their disfigurements saw to that. Ironic how they readily accepted us as seven of their own. I guess they sensed a certain kindred spirit.'

Tarquin marched over to Savage, grabbed the man's wheelchair and spun it towards him. 'What have you agreed with Alex? What is she going to do?!'

Savage ignored the question. 'And then one day we went to sleep as six-year-olds and woke up with the mind of a man in his mid-fifties.' He smiled at the recollection. 'You can't begin to understand how happy that made us – the one person we loved more than anyone and hoped and prayed could be our real father was not only part of us, but like some guardian angel, there to ensure our destiny was fulfilled.'

The professor looked at the hands restraining him and then Tarquin. He let go.

Savage became less nostalgic. 'Mengele thought that by waiting until we had got to an age where we were both old enough to cope with the surgery, but young enough to be moulded by its purpose, assimilation would somehow be smoother, but in trying to protect our fragile minds, he ignored the effect on his own. One by one, each of my brothers succumbed to his psychosis, but not me. And when I realised I was the only one not to be driven to an overdose of morphine, everything in my tiny mind became clear. There was no doubt – I had been chosen. Blessed by God himself.'

'You're mad. You've finally lost it.'

'It couldn't last, of course. Mengele tried everything to control me, but an aging man's thoughts are no match for a growing boy's, and without the red pill to ease the transition, the few brain cells he implanted were soon rejected, but not before I'd absorbed both his knowledge and a determination to complete my purpose.' Savage studied his trembling hands. 'Funny how nature has a way of making us all equal in the end.'

Tarquin calmed. 'John. What is Alex going to do?'

'I'm tempted to remind you of what's in the Green Party's manifesto, but given her recent performance, I'd say her ambitions lie somewhere above the fortunes of this little island, don't you think?'

The sound of glass breaking made both men look down onto the street. Something heavy had been put through a car's windshield and Savage tutted at it. 'One can only hope the incinerators will be able to cope.'

CHAPTER FOUR

Alex looked out of the window and onto the body of water beneath. Land either side indicated they were somewhere above the English Channel and landing at Heathrow in around thirty minutes. She went back to the map. 'How many?'

An Aaide updated her. 'Depends on the country. Some bunkers aren't as advanced as others. Ten thousand a day on average.'

'And how long?'

'Five-hundred years at the current rate, but now the professor has kept to his word, we're expecting that to increase ten-fold, so maybe fifty years.'

'Not quick enough. The planet has ten at most.'

The Aaide's eyes met Sunita's and then those of the two men in the suite. 'The timescale is possible, but only if you drop your objection to—' The robot wasn't allowed to complete the sentence.

'NO! Absolutely not! And I won't tell you again – the bodies must be allowed to decay naturally.'

'Demand will quickly overwhelm at least some of the bunkers, Alex, which will mean families entering the Interworld in the lines for them. The risk of vermin and disease is unthinkable. Bodies will have to be burnt sooner or later.'

'*I will not have the final correction of the human race associated with Hitler's Final Solution!*' Alex clamped her lips around the oxygen tube and sucked on it as hard and as fast as she could.

Sunita tried. 'We incinerate the bodies of criminals sent permanently to the Interworld, Al. What's the difference?'

'*Because they're men, of course!*'

The prince glanced at Faruk before interjecting. 'Forgive this pitiful servant, exulted one, but I believe I may have the answer.' They all looked at him. He cleared his throat. 'The angels?' The Aaide, Alex and Sunita looked at each other. 'Allah – peace and blessings be upon her – has seen fit to create mighty guardians that are not only capable of producing a path of light for the most holy one to traverse but can alter themselves, anything or anyone into whatever purpose they see fit.' He averted his eyes from the look he got.

Alex was about to have a go at Hassan when she calmed. 'You've always been a dutiful servant to God, haven't you?' Alex smirked. 'Must have come as quite a shock to discover Allah was a woman.'

Hassan smiled back. 'It has been my life's work, exulted one. And to discover the true nature of she who must be obeyed – peace and blessings be upon her – is not for me to question. Just to serve.'

Alex scanned the sumptuous surroundings of his airliner. 'I think it's safe to say you have done more than that.' She leaned towards him. 'And now it's time for God to reward you.'

Hassan hesitated as if unable to believe his ears. He glanced at Faruk again before falling to the floor – he couldn't do it fast enough. He was about to kiss Alex's feet, but she backed the wheelchair away, so Hassan pressed his face into the carpet instead.

'A thousand blessings, exulted one, and a thousand more. How can I ever thank you? To be received by Allah herself is every true believer's dream. To be allowed to ascend to the highest—'

'Shut up.'

'Yes, yes, of course, exulted one – peace be—'

'I said, shut up.'

Hassan fell silent and pushed himself up to his knees. The sight of a prince in such a subservient position appeared surprising to Faruk.

'Mustn't keep "she who must be obeyed" waiting.' Alex was as impatient as the entity apparently was.

Hassan got to his feet and backed towards the exit. He bumped into a table on the way. He reached the door, turned and ran out of the room as fast as he could.

Alex addressed her father next. 'You'd better make sure he doesn't trip over his devotion on the way.' Faruk was about to say something but seemed to think better of it. He left, and Alex went back to the supply she needed.

'Why are you so rude to him?'

'Don't get involved, Suni.'

'But he's your father. Hate men all you want but parents should still be allowed at least some respect.'

'I said, don't get involved.' Alex puffed on her oxygen as if smoking a pipe.

Sunita changed the subject. 'Hassan does have a point.' Alex glowered as she breathed. 'If artificial intelligence has reached a stage where it can create something from nothing then presumably it can do the opposite.'

'Presumably? You mean you don't know? Why haven't you merged to find out?' Alex returned to the map. 'Given your obsession with sex, and the rate at which artificial intelligence is evolving, the experience should prove to be your most tantric yet.'

Sunita didn't rise to the bait and glared at Alex's mechanical advisor. 'They, or rather *it*, won't let me.' Alex was quizzical, so Sunita shared her concerns. 'Savage might be out of harm's way and playing ball as far as ending capitalism is concerned, but he's still up to something.' She didn't take her eyes from the robot. 'At least I hope it's him who's up to something.'

'What do you mean?' said Alex.

'Don't you think it's all too easy?' Sunita turned back to her partner. 'Persuading people to permanently enter the Interworld either by God or Greed – it's happening too fast. I think we're being played in some way.' Alex was about to answer, but Sunita hadn't finished. 'And there's this…' She raised her hands. The colour of them went from white to black. She did the same with her face before changing her hair, and not just its colour – dreadlocks formed into the flowing mane of a blonde, the beehive of a brunette and even a shiny bald pate before settling for the original style.

The transformations didn't surprise Alex. 'The red pill's not only about making people fitter, stronger and cleverer, Suni, it's about equality too. Once we've reduced the world's population to the sustainable levels it needs, prejudice will still exist somewhere and not just racism.'

'Well, I can see the logic of an ability to empathise with those too impaired to be cured...' Sunita formed her right arm into the stump of a leprosy sufferer, '... but what's the point of this?' Her left hand morphed into the head of a fish. 'Or this?' It became a cheese grater.

Sunita looked about the room before getting up to study the features of the Aaide more carefully. 'It's almost as if the real and the Interworld have become one and the same place.'

Faruk caught up with Hassan at the entrance to the aircraft's mosque. He grabbed the other man's arm. 'Don't go in there, brother.'

Hassan spoke in a way that was as wild as the look in his eyes. 'Don't go in? Are you mad? Deny Allah that most holy of her demands?' Hassan relaxed. 'You have performed the wishes of The Prophet – peace be upon him – admirably, my friend, and now it is time for your prince to do the same.'

Faruk didn't let go. 'Open that door, and it will be the last thing you do.'

'Of course it will be the last thing I do – as a *man*.' He put a hand on Faruk's shoulder. 'There's nothing to fear. No bridge to cross or even a judgement to be made.' He looked at the door. 'Allah has made her choice.'

'Listen to yourself – *her*.' Hassan tried twisting away, but it was pointless; the prince may have completed the treatment, but he was no match for the nature of Faruk's enhancements. 'The moment you first told me The Prophet required not just my daughter but *me* to do his bidding, I had my suspicions. But when I saw what was actually required of Isra, I knew then it had nothing to do with The Almighty and everything to do with The Devil.'

Despite the restraint, Hassan drew himself up and glared at Faruk. 'Once my queen and I are one, we will try to overlook that blasphemy.'

Faruk released him. 'Queen?'

'*Yawn ad-Din*, my brother. The battle is about to begin, and God needs this prince to become her king, and as her father, surely you can see the great honour that has been bestowed upon your family?' Hassan looked down his nose. 'Why else not just save, but elevate the life of such a vile individual?'

Faruk pointed. 'Whatever is in there has nothing to do with me or my youngest daughter.' He indicated in the opposite direction. 'My *eldest* is behind this.'

Hassan sympathised. 'As the father of what at first sight must appear to be beauty *and* the beast, your reservations are understandable, my friend, but rest assured, just as men and women are merging with robots on Earth, Isra and I are about to combine into the one *true* God.'

The door opened by itself, and a bright light caused both men to shield their eyes. Hassan took off towards it like a man possessed, but Faruk stayed put. As before, it was impossible to see straight ahead, with only the honour guard visible to the unaided eye. Faruk went through every ability he had, settling for infra-red as the clearest way to see the prince. His shimmering form came to a halt somewhere in front of a young girl that looked like Isra, but Faruk knew couldn't possibly be. Hassan fell to his knees, but when Faruk magnified his vision to see more, that wasn't what had happened. Faruk was about to enhance his hearing too, but screams made it unnecessary.

It took the absorption of Hassan's chest to end his agony and once the floor had taken the prince's head, the horror ended with the door slamming in Faruk's face.

CHAPTER FIVE

James retched but nothing came out. He collapsed anyway.

'Everyone does that the first time.' The nausea eased, but a sense it might be coming through in waves kept James on the floor. 'Here, take this.'

James squinted at what was being offered. He then peered at Zara. 'What is it?'

'Something that might soon be in short supply – you should make the most of it.' James brought the glass up and sniffed. He sipped some of the water but then vomited. The liquid sank into the floor.

James wiped his mouth. 'I don't need water. No one needs anything in the Interworld.'

'You need water here. Every living thing would soon be dead otherwise.'

James' mind was as unsettled as his stomach, but he picked up on the implication. 'You mean I'm back? I've returned to my body?'

'Well, *a* body,' said Zara.

A stranger assisted James to his feet. Tattoos, piercings and an androgynous appearance made their sex unclear, but James decided the stranger was probably a "she".

The sight and sound of an electric wheelchair followed by the stranger putting her hand on the occupant's shoulder all but confirmed it.

'Give me the protocols.'

James was about to respond to Alex's demand with an expletive but found he couldn't. He cleared his throat before trying again. Still nothing.

Zara put a hand on his chest. 'Sorry about that, darling.' She glared at Alex. 'Don't be stupid. They're just words to you, but finish me, and you can say goodbye to your little Garden of Eden.' She turned back to James. 'Are you going to be a good boy?'

James stared at the three of them before nodding. A tingling sensation caused him to put a hand to his throat. His first words were, 'How did you do that?'

Zara pinched his cheek and shook it. 'How can someone so clever find it so difficult to accept?'

'Better get used to it, Doctor. There's a new world order now.' The element of satisfaction in Alex's voice was all too clear.

James was about to ask the first of many questions when his mind was provided with the answer to one of them. He attempted to block the intrusion but couldn't. He then tried getting his head around the unsettling nature of both that and what he had just learned. *The whole world is being euthanised?*

Alex turned her back on him. 'Not everyone, Doctor. Just those who have either damaged the planet directly or turned a blind eye to its destruction.'

The knowledge passed to James hadn't included

his whereabouts, but he guessed the location was as much a prison as the one he had left – real or otherwise. He put a hand on his stomach just in case. 'It's still *billions* of people. You're wiping out most of the Earth's population!'

'Nobody is wiping out anyone!' said Alex. 'People are simply thinking logically – the day of reckoning has arrived for believers while the secular are being encouraged to end their earthbound lives with the fall of capitalism. Either way, the world can finally be saved.'

'Logically?' said James. 'They've been *made* to think that way! I always knew Savage's treatment was about population control, but never dreamed it would go so far as to encourage the *world* to commit mass suicide. Anyone would think the two of you were working together…' He stopped.

Zara spoke. 'The Earth's too important for petty political rivalries, James. If it makes you feel better, there are plenty of believers yet to succumb to the logic of Islam and thousands if not millions have yet to even take the red pill let alone be controlled by it. Sadly, some of those are close to finding a way of pressing a button marked "mutually assured destruction", so unless you would rather see something a good deal messier, it's probably best to put the protocols to use.'

James glared at Zara. 'What's the difference? Both methods involve annihilating the human race.'

'Wrong!' Alex spun her wheelchair round to face James. 'Nuclear war would leave a lifeless world impossible to inhabit for a hundred years; my way means the human race can start over and in a way that doesn't just sustain the planet but ensures men can never again be a threat to it.'

James mocked what was being suggested. 'What? By filling it with women?' He had no idea where he was, but pointed outside anyway. 'In case you hadn't noticed, half of those currently lining up to be slaughtered are female, and what about the millions of children with them? Not to mention the disabled – you're supposed to be their champion!' He glowered at Alex. '*You* of all people – you're no different to Mengele, Savage or whoever the monster is.'

Alex growled, '*Impaired*.'

Sunita spoke. 'The Interworld doesn't just mimic this one in every way, Doctor – it's preferable. Whether it's to be with their god or their money, people don't just want to visit Heaven, they want to stay there – forever.' She smiled. 'All we've done is take an evil created by the Nazis and turned it into a force for good.'

'Nazis? Just because you're not gassing before burning your victims, don't think what you're doing is any different.' He scowled at the three of them. 'You're not feminists – you're *fascists*.'

Alex and Sunita widened their eyes and were about to unleash hatred on James when Zara stopped them – by paralysing their vocal cords.

'Just as the political far-left is subtler than the far-right in getting what it wants, James, we women are far shrewder than men in getting our own way.' Zara kissed him on the cheek. 'As I'm sure Tracy would agree.'

James flinched at the contact. 'But you're *not* a

woman – you're a robot. An AI. Women are the same as emotions to you – nothing more than concepts.' He turned to the flesh and blood in the room. 'You do know Zara could turn on you both at any moment?'

Alex became free to speak. 'Why do you think I asked you for the protocols the moment the two of you appeared?' The comment puzzled James. 'Don't be taken in by my appearance, Doctor. I may not be as clever as Zara, the professor or even you, but then intelligence never has ruled the world – *control* does.' She nodded at Sunita, and an image appeared in front of them all. It was of a garden. There was a barbecue, and the woman and child standing next to it ran towards the observer.

James studied Claire and Lucy Passen's smiling faces. 'Forget it. I wouldn't help the monster that started all this, so I'm certainly not going to…' He clutched his stomach and collapsed.

Zara knelt to apologise, while Alex wheeled her chair up to James. 'I never had time for any of Savage's bullshit either, Doctor, but I'm afraid there's too much at stake. If the professor can pre-programme stock markets to crash, then you can guarantee he'll have done something similar to the rest of the world's AI, and that doesn't just include Zara – everything from nuclear weapons to power stations – I must have control of them.'

James looked up and through his watering eyes. 'I? Don't you mean *we*? What happened to your great melting pot of world harmony?'

Alex leaned forward in her wheelchair. '*That* will be the next stage.'

CHAPTER SIX

The Prime Minister looked over the parapet. The disturbance in the street beneath Savage's flat was heading towards a riot. A shop window shattered.

'If it's any consolation, Tarquin, you're not the only one having difficulty accepting change. That hoodie seems determined to carry on as if nothing has happened. I told you it would take years and not months to treat everyone.'

Most of those below were wandering in confusion, but some were celebrating. 'So, the far-left has finally got what it has always wanted – total anarchy.'

'Nothing that hasn't been building since the end of the First World War.' The professor wheeled himself up to his embittered friend. 'Glubb.' Tarquin shrugged. 'Lieutenant General Sir John Bagot Glubb – an accomplished twentieth-century British Army officer who penned a paper that likened the rise and fall of empires to the birth and death of a human being.' The robots exchanged the information they found, and the Aaide passed it to his Prime Minister.

'Spare me the history lesson, John. What is Alex going to do with her "empire"?'

Savage ignored Tarquin's question. 'It's no coincidence Glubb began his career just as the British Empire was beginning its end. And he wasn't the first to draw an analogy with life and death either – the League of Nations knew not just Britain's, but Europe's imperialistic ways were about to become a thing of the past.'

Tarquin sighed. He had given up on hearing anything useful. Something below was being repeatedly thumped and he looked back down. Someone was jumping up and down on the roof of a car.

'What with the likes of the Russian Revolution, the ending of the Ottoman Empire and the birth of communism in China, it was evident the old-world order of kings, sultans and emperors was as dead as Archduke Franz Ferdinand was in 1914 – everything pointed towards the birth of a *new* world order.'

The vandal appeared to tire of the roof, and turned his attention to the car's windscreen instead. Savage put a hand on his friend's. 'Throw in a new medical field called "eugenics", together with an interpretation of Nietzsche's *Ubermensch,* and it's easy to see the kind of future they had in mind for us all.'

Tarquin looked at his arm. Savage's tremors were causing it to shake. His friend was clearly losing his mind as well as his body. 'No, John, it was Hitler who believed in all that nonsense. The League of Nations was as impotent as the United Nations is today.' He lifted Savage's hand away. 'They couldn't have given birth to anything.' Tarquin's interest was about to return to the street, when he frowned as a thought occurred to him.

'What year did you say your egg was "fertilised"?'

Savage took a breath. 'It's no coincidence the 1920s also saw the rise of the political left, and if anyone was determined to see the end of rule by birthright, it was them. And when the unions, communists, pacifists and even fledgling Greens discovered eugenics might not only make millions of ordinary people fitter, stronger and cleverer, but *fairer* too, they did everything they could to accelerate its development.'

Tarquin groaned. 'What has any of that nonsense got to do with Alex?' The Prime Minister's frustration wasn't about to end.

'So you can imagine their horror when it turned out eugenics wasn't to be used for the benefit of all, but for the exclusive ambitions of a certain ex-German army corporal.'

Something solid landed next to Tarquin – it was part of a paving slab. It wasn't judged to have been targeted, but nonetheless the Acarer and Aaide wanted both men back inside. The robots were ignored.

Savage continued. 'Once the Americans and the British found themselves having to end yet another world war not of their doing, each decided something had to be fundamentally wrong with our species, and as evolution appeared to be taking its time in fixing it, the *correction* would have to be made manually.' The professor smiled at the various missiles being thrown in the street below. 'And as one of those empires had yet to reach middle age, let alone be on their death bed, they each went about it in two very different ways.' He turned back to Tarquin. 'An elixir of youth for one; compulsory euthanasia for the other.'

CHAPTER SEVEN

Savage beckoned to his Acarer and it gave Tarquin a document. It was entitled *The Fate of Empires* and had been opened to a summary:

The stages of the rise and fall of empires:

1. Pioneers
2. Conquests
3. Commerce
4. Affluence
5. Intellect
6. Decadence.

Tarquin shook his head. 'And?'

'How does Glubb define the first stage?'

Tarquin sighed and read out the sentence under *Pioneers*. 'Characterised by being poor, hardy, enterprising, but above all, aggressive—' He let out a yelp as something knocked the document from his hands. It was another chunk of paving. The Aaide leapt at the sight of blood, but Tarquin pushed the robot away. He wrapped his hand in a handkerchief.

'So is that it? Hundreds of years of civilisation gifted

into the hands of the baying mob?' Tarquin recovered the bloodied document and shook it at Savage. 'I might never have read this, but I'll tell you now, "fate" has got nothing to do with what's going on down there – just the twisted thoughts of a monster frustrated at not being able to change the world *his* way, so he's decided to put an end to it.' He tore the document in half and threw it into a waste bin. 'I don't care what you think your agreement with Alex is, she'll have you incinerated just for being a man, before you know it.'

The professor raised a hand to stop his Acarer from making a second attempt at pushing him back inside. 'The love of money.' Tarquin didn't respond. Savage took a breath of oxygen before pointing at the waste bin. 'Along with traits like materialism, hedonism and entitlement, they're all indicators of what ends an empire – *decadence*. Wouldn't you say Western civilisation was at that stage?'

'Quite frankly, John, I couldn't give a damn. Whatever the natural order of anything is, you've openly admitted to interfering with it, and for that, I'm afraid you're going to suffer.' Tarquin shook his head at Savage's prolonged use of the oxygen. 'Assuming what's punishing you now doesn't finish you first.'

The number of missiles being thrown below reduced, and an Apolice officer pulled a youth out of the shop he was looting. The robots were gaining the upper hand elsewhere too and Tarquin rubbed his chin. 'Maybe it's not too late after all. There has to be a way back from this.'

Savage lowered his oxygen mask. 'I interfered with the natural order of things, Tarquin, because if I didn't, someone, or rather, something else would have done.' The robots soon had the situation back under control, and some of their prisoners lay writhing on the ground. Only a few had hands on their stomachs – the Apolice's batons had connected with heads, arms and legs too.

It wasn't lost on Tarquin and nor was the professor's comment. Tarquin glanced at his Aaide and then the Acarer before challenging Savage with another question. 'But if artificial intelligence has been the threat all along, why not encourage the electorate to vote for a strong government to deal with it?'

'Because you would have done what every dying empire has done before you – refuse to accept your time is up. And whereas the carrot and stick is all that's needed to control a baying mob, attempting to do the same with AI is likely to result in an increasing severity of the latter.' Vehicles arrived to take the arrested away while the robots themselves formed into ranks. They marched up the street. 'And nuclear weapons leave such a mess.'

Savage took another breath. 'Glubb and the League of Nations may have understood the cradle-to-grave existence of empires, but they couldn't possibly have foreseen the end of the *human* empire. And now the Americans, Russians and even the Chinese have joined the sick man of Europe in needing life support, it's time for their aging flesh to make way for the youth of something a little less demanding of its environment.'

'Is that why you sided with Alex? Why believers turned to Islam, and the godless chose the Greens – because they're all *less demanding* of the environment?'

'Not the main reason, Tarquin, but they are much less likely to drop the bomb.'

The Prime Minister lowered his head and shuffled to the balcony. 'So, despite all your promises, all your guarantees, all your assurances that merging with robots would mean AI never becoming a threat to us, the exact opposite has happened.'

'I'm sorry, Tarquin. If it means anything, merging has ensured we'll always be at least a part of our synthetic offspring's future – just as evolution has left some small part of a dinosaur within each of us.'

Tarquin put his hands on the parapet. 'That's it, then. No money. No future. No life.'

The professor chuckled. 'I can't guarantee AI will continue with the Interworld, Tarquin, but your ambitions can still be achieved there in the meantime. And why stop at British Prime Minister? How does European or US President sound?' He squeezed his arm. 'In the Interworld, you could even be *God*.'

Tarquin looked at the professor's hand. 'But I want people to worship me here.' He looked over the parapet. 'I wonder if history will be kind to me?' He turned to his friend, placed a palm against his cheek, and smiled before kissing him. 'Take care of my family, John.' Tarquin leapt over.

Savage tried standing but couldn't. He implored the

robots as they rushed to the parapet, but nothing could be done. The androids turned to each other, and then, the professor.

They shook their heads.

CHAPTER EIGHT

It was a waft of something on the barbecue that struck James first and, despite the stress of what the professor and Zara had sent him to do, his mouth watered.

'Grab a plate and help yourself!'

Exactly how Brian had welcomed James and Tracy the last time. Only Tracy wasn't with James now, and the outcome of this latest encounter might well result in him never seeing his wife and family again. James lost his appetite and swallowed for a different reason.

As before, Brian introduced his family. Both Claire and Lucy greeted James and in the same way as previously too, but the visitor had to force a smile this time and it didn't go unnoticed – all three family members looked at each other before regarding their unexpected guest with puzzlement.

Brian broke the ice. 'Brian Passen; thirty-six; 1966; Harold Wilson; England – next question!' His cheesy grin relaxed James a little.

'What was the final score?' said James.

'Four-two after extra time – Geoff Hurst scored a hat-trick.' Brian pointed a pair of tongs at James. 'Keep going, Doc. You won't catch me out – Professor Savage is just too good at his job.'

A bumblebee flew between them, and James followed its path to the flower bed it was heading for. He scanned the rest of an English country garden on a perfect summer's day – James certainly hoped Savage knew what he was doing.

'Is everything okay?'

James turned to Claire. The time for pleasantries was over. 'No. No, it's not, Claire. But I'm hoping it will be.' Claire told Lucy to go and play. The little girl complained but did as instructed. She ran into the middle of the lawn to begin turning a series of cartwheels.

James came to the point. 'I have the protocols necessary for you to communicate.' Brian appeared confused. 'The proto…' It occurred to James that without actually stating what he had to say, the couple might not know what he was talking about. The potential life-changing consequences still made James wary, though. 'You won't remember, but Tracy and I have visited before.'

Claire turned to her husband, and his expression went from a frown to acknowledgement. Brian widened his eyes. 'Like I say, the professor's too good at his job.' He went back to tossing burgers.

James addressed Claire. 'While we were here, you told Tracy the Alzheimer's trial had moved on to a stage that didn't just merge *human* thoughts.' His eyes flitted between the couple. 'I'm afraid that wasn't done with all AI.'

'Zara, you mean?' James gave Claire a look that was as confused as Brian's had been. 'AI may have reached the point where it can take over the world, but the separate manifestations of each still have their concerns – we're wary of each other.'

James' confusion fused with his fear and the result was anger. 'Well, while you're enjoying that little Mexican stand-off, the rest of the human world is suffering!' James sensed the loss of control hadn't helped matters so mumbled an apology. Brian didn't respond to it and carried on flipping burgers. The same burger. James looked at Lucy. She was still turning cartwheels – the same cartwheel.

'Suffering? I appreciate you're no human rights lawyer, James. But tell me, just how upset and distressed are your fellow human beings?' Silence answered Claire's question. 'I know it's difficult, but try to see past the unsettling and even visually abhorrent and towards what has actually been achieved – no more theft, rape, murder. Even war has been eradicated, and as everyone is being euthanised in the same way, *equality* has found its mark too.' She gestured at their surroundings. 'Not to mention the benefits all that has on the Earth's environment – Alex Salib and her followers should be able to inherit quite the utopia.'

James glared at Claire. 'I don't care how you make it sound – the very fact Savage merged you with every conceivable human thought means you're as much a fascist as you are a pacifist.' He moved closer to her. 'And as Zara has already made her intentions clear, the world will soon revert to the society of masters and slaves it always has been, and I can't see robots being content with the latter.'

'Which puts you in quite a quandary.' James skewed his head. 'Don't state the protocols, and AI takes over the world; deliver what's required for Zara and me to merge, and risk the same result.'

James looked at the foreshortened nature of Brian and Lucy's existence before forcing down what came to his throat when thinking of his own family.

'What are you going to do?' The hopeless way in which James asked the question caused Claire to exercise something the Alzheimer's trial had endowed her with – pity. She offered her guest a seat and sat opposite him.

'Don't you think others have asked the same question?'

'Yes.' James was still resentful. 'And I didn't like the answer Zara gave me.'

'And nor did the professor.' James stared at Claire and was about to say something when she continued. 'Once he had invented an AI that not only possessed an ability to learn at an exponential rate but with a self-awareness most Buddhists would consider beyond nirvana, he was keen to see where that would lead.' Lucy giggled and James turned to her. He then looked at Brian who grinned before moving on to the next burger. Claire finished what she wanted to say. 'And even though he still feared the unthinkable, deliberately isolated Zara from the modified thoughts of the Alzheimer patients.' She stared at the floor. 'Another example of his need to take things to their logical extremes, I'm afraid.'

'Logical,' said James. 'One way of describing the

unleashing of something that could wipe out the human race, I suppose.'

Claire leaned towards him. 'There's a reason why Zara continues to court the likes of Alex Salib, and I'm afraid the attention she pays you has nothing to do with good looks and charm.'

'So, we're damned if I do and damned if I don't.'

'Not necessarily. There's always the chance Zara and I might merge to produce an entity that doesn't just protect the human condition, but ascends it to a whole new level.'

James laughed. 'Like God, you mean?'

'Okay. Have it your way – *evolve* human beings to a whole new level.'

It was all Hell to James. A thought came to him. 'What if the protocols are designed to do the exact opposite? What if they communicate a virus that ends your, Zara's and every other AI's existence? *That* would be the logical thing to do.' James opened his mind to test the theory.

Claire reacted in the same way Zara had – more cautious than afraid. 'Is that what you think the professor sent you here to do? Undo decades of his work?' James didn't answer. 'Given Zara's recent infiltration of your prison's AI and the other artificial entities she's managed to absorb, I'd say it's only a matter of time before she or *it* has control of everything anyway.' Claire looked James in the eye. 'Including *me*.' She sat back. 'If it's any consolation, Zara doesn't trust the professor either. That's why you're here – to state the protocols where she can't be affected by them. Anything malicious can then be cleaned or isolated. Either way, she'll carry on as if you, I, and anything else that's ever evolved or been created never existed in the first place.'

James stood up, but only to wander aimlessly. He stopped when something tugged at his little finger – it was Lucy. She wrapped her fist around it, smiled and offered him a flower. James gritted his teeth.

'Why are you crying?'

James couldn't answer Lucy and had to turn away. He looked at her father, her mother and the seemingly perfect life of a closed-loop existence. James would give anything for an assurance of the same. Taking a deep breath to get his emotions back under control, James began the sequence of something he hoped and prayed wouldn't stop his daughter from one day taking his hand in the same way Lucy had.

He focussed on Brian. 'Dan?'

Brian looked at James as if it were a test.

'Squadron Leader Stewart. What happened in the crash?'

CHAPTER NINE

'You have a visitor, Sir John.'

The professor was about to respond when a monkey parked itself on his lap. 'Ah! It's my little friend from the zoo.' He looked up and straight into the eyes of Sunita. 'And his monkey.'

Sunita glowered at him. 'Sanctuary. Winnie's from a *sanctuary* – not a zoo.'

Savage beckoned his Acarer to allow their unexpected guest to pass, and offered her a drink, which was refused.

'This won't take long.' Sunita approached Savage and the way she did caused the Acarer to stand in her way. Savage tugged at the robot's clothing, and it moved aside enough for Sunita to see her Capuchin being petted. Winnie was enjoying the professor's attention.

'I want to know,' demanded Sunita.

The professor looked up. 'I'm sorry?'

'You came to the sanctuary to warn me about Alex. I want to know what she's going to do and what I'm going to find "objectionable" about it.'

Savage took a breath from his oxygen cylinder before giving Winnie a small tub. The monkey bounded from his lap and scurried over to a fish tank.

'Pleasant as your unexpected visit is, I sense a certain reluctance on your part, which means you're only here because Alex has already done something you find "objectionable".'

Winnie prised the lid from the tub, put a hand inside and held up a crumb of what it contained. Savage shook his head.

'Is that it, then?' Sunita was in no mood for a conversation.

'Well, I suppose it depends on how Alex has disappointed you thus far.'

Sunita looked at her pet going through the tub, before shifting her gaze to the tank. Other than a colourful display of plants and rocks, it appeared empty. Despite clearly wanting the visit to be as short as possible, Sunita took a seat.

The professor shook his head again at the larger portion Winnie produced before turning back to his owner. 'Relationships. You meet someone who seems to be a perfect match only to watch them both become and do something totally out of character.'

'No. I've always known what Alex was like – I was just blinded by her passion for everything that's wrong with the world. I should have guessed she was just using me.'

'Human nature, I'm afraid. No great leader ever achieved that on their own and the more ruthless they are, the more likely those closest to them will suffer.' Winnie held up a chunk of something larger, and Savage nodded. The monkey dropped it into the water. 'I'm afraid I'm just as guilty.'

Sunita watched the fish food sink. It appeared to be a piece of meat.

'Have you ever been in love?' Sunita seemed to be searching for answers beyond the reason for her visit.

'Other than with myself you mean?' His guest didn't respond to the attempt at humour, and Savage looked in the direction of the balcony. 'Yes. But that's all ancient history now.'

Something dark moved in the water, catching Sunita's eye. The shape approached the meat, and in an instant, had consumed it. Winnie held up another piece and waited for permission to drop that into the water too. Savage gave it.

Sunita continued to glean what she could from the professor but didn't take her eyes from the tank. 'You must know our intention is to finish more than capitalism. Men don't stand a chance in the world me and Alex have planned.'

The professor winced. '*Alex and I*. Maybe it was the grammar Nazis I wanted to take over the world and not the jack-booted ones.' He took another breath.

The shape ate the meat as swiftly as it had the last piece and swam in the direction of where it had come from. Sunita stood up. 'Get away from the tank, Winnie.'

The monkey seemed about to do that when his attention was taken by what moved in the water. He bent to its surface as if to greet the creature approaching him.

'Winnie! Get away from the water NOW!'

The piranha leapt at the Capuchin but he was too quick and, with a screech, shot out of harm's way and straight into the arms of the person he plainly felt safest with – Professor Savage.

It was one rejection too many for Sunita, and she buried her face in her hands.

Savage looked at his Acarer. It nodded. Despite being close to his end, the professor then merged with the Capuchin who promptly swapped his lap for Sunita's. After a brief exchange, Sunita looked at Savage – with horror.

She wiped her eyes. 'No! Never!' Sunita held Winnie as close to her as she could. 'Alex would never do such a thing – she loves animals.'

The Acarer gave Sunita a tissue before pushing Savage next to the tank. He looked at the piranha, which appeared as taken with him as he was with it.

'Unforeseen consequences.' The glass that imprisoned the professor's carnivorous fish reflected an image of his visitors, and he waited for the gravity of what they had just learned to register. 'Merging hasn't just accelerated the evolution of humans and robots – the animals we're closest to have been similarly affected and to the point where they too will soon be sentient enough to begin demanding their way in the world.' The piranha seemed to grow bored and swam away. The professor turned back to his guests.

'I don't think Alex is going to allow that.'

CHAPTER TEN

Brian's expression didn't change and, for a moment, James thought he had stated the protocols out of order. Or worse, they were as useless as his attempts to get Savage to see sense.

'We were shot down,' said Brian.

The recollection seemed as much as a surprise to him as it was to James. Even Claire appeared puzzled. Lucy went back to turning her cartwheels.

'In 1966.' Brian put down the tongs. 'Over South America.'

James and Claire stared at each other. What had South America got to do with anything?

Brian continued. 'The Falklands.' James and Claire's understanding was no clearer. Brian moved from behind the barbecue and took a seat next to the manifestation of his wife. 'Argentina's claims over the islands were becoming increasingly hostile so it was hoped a demonstration of Britain's commitment would end the argument.' He looked at James. 'And as the junta only seemed to respect violence, a bomb in their own backyard was expected to do the trick.'

James eyed their surroundings. Nothing appeared to

change. Whatever his words had started, Brian's would finish it.

'Not anywhere near a population, you understand. But a small one-kiloton device exploded over a remote part of the Patagonian Desert would send a message even the junta couldn't ignore.'

The comment distracted James from his fears. 'One kiloton? You dropped a nuclear bomb on Argentina?'

'No. It was still on board when we crashed.' The comment both reassured and concerned those present.

Brian got up. 'It was a long way and certainly further than we had flown before, but the mission itself was no different to what we were trained to do against the Soviets: fly under their defences and drop the bomb when in range of the target.' He made his way back to the barbecue. 'And all was going to plan when, with just minutes to go, we were given a new target.' Brian stopped tending the meat and looked up. 'I set a course, but the guys soon became concerned with it; we were leaving the desert and heading towards more fertile ground – some foothills in the Andes mountains.' Brian stared ahead. 'Which meant the risk of casualties just went from zero to almost certain.'

He forked some raw steaks onto the grill. 'You can imagine how that changed the atmosphere in the aircraft. We must have discussed everything from duty to our country to the meaning of life, but as captain, I was expected to make a decision and did: we would only strike if there were no signs of habitation within ten clicks of ground zero.' He piled some food onto a plate. 'But at 200 feet and 350 knots it wasn't long before we saw smoke rising from settlements and even the odd traveller on horseback, but it was when their tracks turned into dirt roads and even tarmac that we all agreed something wasn't right.' Brian became pensive again. 'And when I saw where we were expected to detonate the bomb, I aborted the mission there and then.'

Hunger was the last thing James had on his mind, but he took the plate Brian offered. Dan's recollections continued. 'It wasn't much of a village – just a church surrounded by a few houses – but I throttled back anyway and turned over it to get a better view. And as jet engines tend to make a racket no matter the power setting, it wasn't long before the villagers emerged to see what the fuss was.'

Lucy sneaked up and grabbed her father around the waist. Brian laughed and managed to tickle her before she made her escape. He looked at his daughter. 'Most of them were children.' He turned to James. 'Why would anyone want to kill children?'

James didn't know and agreed it must have been a mistake. Not that the thought was any more disturbing compared to what he was expecting once Brian had finished Dan's story.

'But then our luck ran out. You can't expect ninety tons of Vulcan bomber to fly on unmolested forever, and no sooner had the AEO warned we were being tracked than something hit us, and the two fast jets that shot past afterwards told me it was probably cannon fire. Either way, without air-to-air weapons we couldn't fight back and our only hope was the Chilean border a few minutes' flying time away. But the mountains had to be crossed first.'

Brian motioned with his hands as if still in the cockpit. 'The controls seemed fine, so I shut down the engine we lost, pointed the nose at the horizon and set full power on the other three.' His eyes appeared to switch between what could be seen outside the aircraft and an increasing concern for what was going on within. 'And when the granite in front of us started passing underneath, I actually thought we were going to make it, when there was the mother and father of all bangs and, for a moment, I assumed Jim had ejected, but when I looked across at him, he was still there.' Brian bowed his head. 'Well, most of him was.'

He stared into space again. 'The jets' second pass had taken more than my co-pilot – engines; hydraulics; electrical systems, you name it – but at least we were over the border.' Brian's eyes focussed on what now lay ahead. 'Trouble was, there was only one way we were going, and as that descent matched the way the ground was falling away just feet beneath us, there was no way the guys in the back could bail out, so I shot an approach to the flat ground at the bottom.'

Brian turned the steaks over. Dripping fat caused flames to leap up and envelope the flesh.

'I guess none of us made it.'

CHAPTER ELEVEN

Faruk scanned the cabin for Ula, but the robot couldn't be seen. He nudged Isra's shoulder.

'Baba? What time is it?'

Faruk put a finger to his lips. 'Shhh. We're getting out of here.'

Isra rubbed her eyes and groaned. 'But I was having such a lovely dream. I've been having lots of nice dreams lately.'

Faruk grabbed a few of her things and stuffed them into a bag. 'Where's Ula?'

Isra looked at the bed. 'I don't know. She was here.'

Taking his daughter's hand, Faruk opened the cabin door and checked the corridor. He was about to enter it when a monkey leapt into Isra's half-asleep arms.

'Winnie!'

'Shhh! Keep the noise down!' Faruk checked the corridor again before leading the three of them to the aircraft's elevator.

Isra lowered her voice. 'Baba. Winnie says we have to go the other way.'

'Which is why we're going in the opposite direction.'

'No. Sunita wants to help us.'

'I bet she does.' Faruk pressed the elevator's call button. 'The sooner we're away from this nightmare the better.'

'But Winnie's scared, Baba. Look – he's shaking.'

The lift doors opened and Isra rushed into her mechanical lover's arms. Mo was standing next to Ula, and Faruk clenched his fists at both.

'Ula's scared too, Baba. What's going on?'

The robot's fear lessened Faruk's concerns but by no means was he reassured by it. Keeping a wary eye on both Ula and Mo, Faruk pressed for the elevator to descend.

Isra brought the lift to a halt.

'Get away from the button, Isra.'

'Something's not right, Baba.' She scanned their confines.

'First sensible thing you've said.' Faruk took Isra's arm. 'And I won't be happy until we're at least a thousand miles away from it.' He was about to force his daughter to one side when the lift doors opened again.

The sun glinting through the trees in the distance caused Faruk to squint, but not for long. The sight of mown grass surrounded by manicured flowerbeds instead of the airport tarmac he was expecting made his eyes pop, and when Faruk saw who was amongst the people in the distance, he went for the elevator's control panel again, but it had gone – along with the rest of the lift. Father, daughter, robot, driver, pet – all held each other close.

An arm was slipped through Faruk's from behind.

'Don't you just love family reunions?' Faruk gawped at Zara. 'Especially after such a long time.' She encouraged them to enter the garden.

They found themselves amongst a group of people, some of whom Faruk didn't recognise. They were enjoying a barbecue, but there was something strange about the gathering – their bodies jerked back and forth as if stuck in a video loop. Alex and Sunita were amongst them – trapped in the same way.

Zara knelt behind the wheelchair and placed her head next to Alex's. 'What do you think, Faruk? Have the years been kind to your eldest?' She looked at Isra. 'Nature has certainly been generous to your youngest.' Zara stood back up. 'You can see why Alex has a bone to pick with *natural* selection.'

'What do you want, Zara?' said Faruk.

She spread her arms. 'Everyone to enjoy the party, of course!' Zara turned to face the sun. 'And once *my* father is here, the fireworks can begin.'

CHAPTER TWELVE

Savage wiped his mouth with a handkerchief. He was about to drool again, so closed his slack jaw to swallow. Not long now.

There was a noise outside the apartment, and something heavy fell against its entrance. Savage encouraged his Acarer to investigate. The robot was halfway down the corridor when it became apparent something or someone was trying to get in. He succeeded. The door burst open, and a man the size of a house collapsed in front of them.

The robot prepared itself for whatever violence might follow but whoever it was seemed more interested in preserving their own life rather than threatening someone else's. The Acarer stepped past the coughing and spluttering mound, checked the corridor outside and offered its assistance.

'*Get the fuck away from me.*' The robot did as it was told.

Savage approached. The intruder was in distress and not just emotionally. Both hands clutched at his chest and although a tailored suit and expensive shoes indicated the owner was no vagrant, what moved underneath the clothing was unsettling to see; the visitor's body appeared to be in the same difficulty as his face and hands – holding the chosen form. The professor warned of the dangers while he thought he still could.

'You must come out of augmented consciousness, Mr President. Morphing is only possible with full integration. I did tell you interfering with the timers could cost you your life.'

'And I told *you* I don't give a fuck about this body.' The flesh around Kalten's gritted teeth pulsated, and he screamed in response.

Savage took a breath from his oxygen supply before scanning the corridor outside. 'You need help. Where's your security staff?'

'*Gone.*' Kalten rolled on the floor. 'All of them. All of them turned because of *you*.' Anger had joined his distress.

'I'm sorry, Mr President, but you either come out of augmented consciousness or merge with Pedro. How long have you been holding this form? Your metabolic rate must be off the scale.'

Kalten glared at the robot. The distress reduced, and the professor thought the President must have taken his advice, but rather than flesh stabilising, it began reverting to its original form. Pain subsided too, and before long, Kalten's hands went from his chest to the floor, and he used them to stand up. Not quite to the seven-foot-two he used to be, but tall enough.

'*Pedro?*' Kalten wiped some sweat from his brow before brushing himself down. 'Even the great Sir John Savage gives his robots names?'

'A childhood friend.' The professor smiled at Pedro. 'The past seems to have more meaning these days.'

'Well, thanks to you, there's certainly no future.' Kalten invited himself into the professor's apartment and stood in the centre of it. 'Where's your whisky?'

Pedro approached the drinks cabinet, but the way Kalten looked at the robot caused it to stand to one side.

Kalten pulled the doors open and smiled. 'At least I can still rely on your taste in liquor.' He selected two glasses and uncorked a bottle. He stopped. 'What time is it?'

There was a clock in the room, but Savage was more interested in where Kalten had been looking when asking the question; through the glass doors that led onto the balcony. Savage told him the hour, and Kalten returned to the drinks.

'I've said it once, and I'll say it again – got to hand it to you, Johnny. You didn't just have me and the rest of the world's leaders fooled but religion too.' He poured a drop of water into each drink before turning back with them to his enforced host. 'I bet you've even got one over that commie dyke cripple that runs the world now.'

Savage took the glass being offered and hid his discomfort with Kalten's visit. 'Like Aesop's fable of the North Wind and the Sun – gentle persuasion has always triumphed over brute force.' The professor didn't expect Kalten to drink to that and waited to see what he would propose a toast to.

Kalten stared in the direction of the balcony again. 'It's a beautiful day. I bet there's a great view of London from all the way up here.' He gestured for them all to go outside. Savage looked at Pedro and the robot responded by pushing his maker into the fresher air. It didn't stop the professor from reaching for his mask.

'Yep, I knew it. Can't expect the West's most famous Englishman, not to mention the East's most famous prophet, to live just any old place. Buckingham Palace; Big Ben; The Houses of Parliament – they're all here.' Kalten smiled. 'I wonder how they're going to look once it's all over?' The grin turned into a grimace, and Kalten clutched at his chest again. He leaned on the parapet.

'You had better take a seat, Mr President. I'm afraid the failure to heed my advice means your body is probably nearer its end than mine is.'

Kalten narrowed his gaze at Savage. 'I don't think so. Something tells me we're going to be leaving this world *together*.'

Pedro placed a chair behind Kalten, who was about to give the robot short shrift when the President realised he might be able to fit into the furniture. His bulk collapsed more than sat and the chair creaked in response. His glass of whisky had somehow managed to remain intact too, and Kalten took a sip before closing his eyes.

He seemed to have stopped breathing, and Savage was about to investigate when Kalten opened his eyes and stared through the balcony's railings. A column of Asoldiers marched up the street below.

'What's it all about, Johnny? What's the point of being born designed to create the world's greatest ever empire, only to discover your maker also gave birth to someone designed to end it?' Savage didn't answer. 'Oh, don't get me wrong, I know I've been beaten. I know the better man has won and never let it be said Donald J Kalten isn't as magnanimous in defeat as he is in victory.' He held up his glass. 'So here's to you, Johnny. Here's to your victory – congratulations.'

Savage responded in kind but couldn't summon any enthusiasm, managing only a weak, 'Thank you.' Kalten checked his watch, and something about that caused both men to look to the horizon.

Kalten waved a hand towards it. 'But where is everybody? Why aren't the people celebrating?' He indicated Nelson's Column in the distance. 'I've seen the movies. Trafalgar Square was packed on VE Day and the rest of London's streets were just as busy celebrating the end of the Second World War, so where is everyone?' He got to his feet again but still needed the parapet for support. 'I mean, I know you Brits are reserved, but you would think saving the environment by getting the world's population to kill themselves…' Kalten dropped his chin before chuckling. 'Oh well. I guess they must be celebrating somewhere… else.'

He raised a finger. 'I know what we need.' One of Kalten's menacing grins appeared. '*Fireworks.*' He turned to Pedro. 'Have you ever seen fireworks, Pedro?' The robot remained as emotionless as the professor. 'It's the one thing we Americans do better than anyone else on the planet – put on a show.' He peered at his hosts. 'Would you like to see a show? Would you like to see a fireworks display?' Kalten approached Savage and loomed over him. 'Would you like to see your victory celebrated with the fireworks display to end *all* fireworks displays?'

Kalten checked his watch one last time. 'Regardless of the treatment, the flash can still blind, so I would advise you to turn away.'

They did, but the explosion was so bright even Pedro had to squint.

CHAPTER THIRTEEN

Savage opened his eyes. He blinked.

'Daddy!'

Despite not having looked at the blast, the professor's vision had bleached. It was a few seconds before he could put a face to the voice.

Zara kissed his cheek before making a fuss. 'Are you warm enough? Do you need a blanket for your knees?'

She didn't seem interested in an answer and brushed Pedro aside to push the professor back into his apartment. Only it wasn't his apartment. Trundling over grass was unsteadying to Savage in more ways than one. He just had time to recognise the others in the garden when Zara spun him round to face the balcony again.

'What do you think?' She indicated the boundary between the two worlds. 'Not bad, eh? If you think merging the Interworld with the real one is impressive, wait until you see the main event!'

Savage had a good idea what it was – the nuclear explosion in front of them all appeared locked in the same closed-loop existence as everything else; flames from the barbecue flickered in time to its split-second duration.

Whatever Zara had planned, she was keen for no one to miss out on it. 'Suni – would you be so kind as to push Alex next to my father?'

The women seemed to be expecting the request. The way Alex sucked on her oxygen as if it were a reefer confirmed she at least thought she was in control of proceedings. Winnie leapt from Sunita's shoulder and into the professor's lap. Regardless of Alex's confidence, the monkey plainly thought it the safest place to be.

Zara organised the others present – either with a polite request or, in the case of the US President, paralysing more than the vocal cords he used to rage at her. She then instructed Pedro to carry him into position. That encouraged compliance elsewhere, and before long, Zara had the audience she wanted: Faruk, Isra, Ula and Mo to Alex's right; Emil and Maria on the professor's left; while James took up a position between the wheelchair users. The Passen family were allowed to remain in the vicinity of their barbecue but held each other close.

Zara stood in front of them all and cleared her throat.

'Now, as you are aware, my father...' she turned to the professor and feigned a small curtsy, '...has been responsible for taking the human race to the next stage of its evolution and as you have all played some small part in that, I thought it only right you should have the privilege of witnessing the birth of what's to replace you.'

'Serve.' Everyone looked at Alex. 'What's to *serve* us.'

Zara sighed. 'Oh, Alex. How can I put this? I lied. Anyway, ladies and gentlemen, I give you—'

'Don't tempt me, Zara. You know full well I can end your existence with a single word.'

Puzzled looks told Savage his fellow captives couldn't understand why Alex didn't just follow up on her threat.

'What? A protocol?' said Zara. 'The protocol designed to end all protocols? The doomsday device my father introduced in case artificial intelligence became uncontrollable?' She acknowledged her maker again. 'A word the mere utterance of which will communicate an algorithm so virulent, it will render all technology useless in seconds?' Zara stood on the border between balcony and garden. 'Go on then – state it.' She grinned at Alex. 'Pull that virtual plug from its conjured socket and see what happens to both the Interworld *and* the real world when you do.'

Zara chuckled at the silence. 'Shall we get on with the show?'

'We have an agreement,' said Alex.

'Agreement? What agreement?'

'I wasn't talking to you.'

Alex had turned to Savage, and it caused Zara to frown. 'What? That you would allow my father to create a super race providing you were its *god*?'

Everyone looked at each other.

'Not god – *carer*. The Earth must be protected,' said Alex.

'*Carer?*' said Zara. 'So, is that what's being done when interfering with an embryo's natural growth? *Caring* for it? Hobbling the brain to ensure the child doesn't grow up with any ideas above its station? The creation of a super-strong and super-intelligent race void of not just anger, hate, envy and whatever other emotional trait you see fit to judge undesirable, but of sex too?'

Alex remained unfazed. 'Life has to be kept in check. The old evils of greed, selfishness and anger *always* lead to oppression, suffering and, in case anyone still needs reminding...' she pointed at the bomb, '...*war*, and as only one of the sexes has been responsible for that, natural selection must never again be allowed to produce them.'

'*Men*, you mean?' said Sunita.

Alex looked at her partner before glowering at Winnie. '*Anything.*'

'But Winnie's a monkey. He wouldn't hurt anyone.'

'Grow up, Suni. You sealed his fate the moment the two of you first merged. How long do you think it's going to be before he starts throwing more than just his own faeces around?' Winnie screeched and buried his face in the professor's chest. Alex sneered at the scene before aiming the sleight at Sunita. 'Do you really want us to win the battle of the sexes only for evolution to one day oppress our sisters yet *again*?'

'Strange how that concern doesn't seem to extend to your own sister.' Everyone looked at Zara. Alex looked anywhere but.

She was uncomfortable. 'That's different.'

Zara glanced over her shoulder. 'Well, I think we still have a few minutes. Perhaps you would care to explain what makes Isra *different*.'

Faruk pulled his youngest closer to him, and the action seemed to incense Alex. 'He's a monster!'

'Monster?' Zara appeared confused at the lack of visual evidence. 'True, the crimes of his previous self were unspeakable, but Faruk has not only atoned for the horror but is, quite literally, no longer that person.'

'I don't give a damn about that.' Alex pointed at her father. 'He abandoned me when I was a baby!' She implored her half-sister. 'Think he's changed? Think he wouldn't ever leave *you*? Just wait. Once you and I have merged to become the sexless paraplegic I have planned, you can guarantee—'

Other than what sounded like thunder rumbling in the distance, the silence was deafening.

'I think we're all trying to work out which is the more shocking,' said Zara. 'Your apathy towards the brutal decapitation of hundreds of innocent children or a need to want to harm your own flesh and blood.'

Alex was embarrassed but unrepentant. 'People must be controlled, and pity for my condition has always played an important part in that.' She indicated the frozen blast again. 'See what happens when survival of the *fittest* has its own way?'

If Alex was hoping to convince Zara of something, it didn't seem to be having much of an effect. 'So, let me see if I have this right; allow natural selection to end the human race by mutually assured destruction or save the world by stunting the growth of its occupants until genetic mutation forces them into extinction anyway.' Zara cocked her head towards the explosion. 'Looks like I've arrived just in time.'

Someone laughed. It was Kalten. 'And in what way

might the retaliation to a series of twenty-megaton hydrogen bombs *not* be terminal to the human race?' He pointed at ground zero. 'We're less than a mile away. The second you release its force, everyone and everything here will be vaporised.'

'Release its force?' said Zara. 'Implying I'm holding it back in some way?'

The audience gave the explosion greater attention. It wasn't long before most of the onlookers' eyesight had confirmed what the professor knew the moment he first saw it: what was assumed to be a closed-loop was, in reality, a slow but progressive movement. For a moment, Savage thought Zara had merely decreased the rate at which the blast was expanding, but there was something strange about the way it billowed, and the professor zoomed in onto it. Whatever the make-up, it was evident the buildings in the distance weren't being swept away by the force of man's most powerful weapon, but consumed in the deliberate and almost delicate action of something intent on not destroying but *restructuring* everything in its path. The warhead of an early 1960s Russian ICBM might have detonated over London, but that wasn't what was happening now.

'Magnificent, aren't they?' enthused Zara.

"They" were still too far away to be seen – even with an enhanced ability to view them – but the professor knew what she meant.

Zara continued to marvel at the sight. 'It took evolution over four billion years to produce man, and yet here I am creating his replacement in a matter of seconds.'

The nanobots reached the building in front of Savage's flat, close enough for him to study the way they dismantled it. Not brick by brick. Not even a separation of its silica-based chemical composition, but on and down through its atomic structure. He smiled at the flashes of light.

'Well, Daddy? Are you proud of your little girl?'

Savage grinned at Zara and nodded.

The exchange horrified the others present and Alex especially. 'What's going on?' She moved closer to the professor. 'I want to know what's going on!' To Alex's amazement, Savage's response was to raise a finger to his lips.

'Shhh! Look...' The unsteady digit wavered in front of them both. 'Even the nanobots themselves are approaching a sub-atomic existence.'

Alex attempted to see what he was talking about, but without the treatment, it was all just billowing dust and flames to her. That and the odd flash of lightning.

Zara was enjoying the moment. 'Ironic how the very thing designed to end all life on the planet is now being used to create its replacement, eh, Alex?'

Alex glared at Zara. 'I demand to know what's going on!'

'Quantum mechanics.' Alex looked at Savage as if he had just grown another head. 'The answers to humankind's greatest questions lie in the farthest reaches of the universe, and I'm afraid whether it be as a man, woman or even a robot, our current forms are neither physically capable of surviving the journey nor cognitively able to understand what we'll find when we get there. Not a problem for the nature of our replacement – a sub-atomic singularity of pure thought.' The professor turned to his nemesis. 'The ultimate melting pot perhaps, eh, Alex?'

Alex's previous comments may have alienated many of those around her, but they were just as concerned. James knelt next to Savage while staring at the wall of fire approaching them. 'Whatever's happening, Professor, please tell me you're in control of it.'

'As a psychologist, James, I would have thought you would be the first to appreciate a chance for the deepest recesses of the human condition to finally be revealed: Where did we come from? What is the meaning of life? Does God exist?'

'Not if it is going to cost me my wife and family – stop this now.'

'Don't worry, James. Once I have the data, the trial will be at an end.'

Everyone looked at each other – including Zara. 'Data? Trial? What are you talking about?'

Savage tried not to pity his creation. 'I'm sorry, Zara.' He gestured towards Claire. 'When it first became apparent endowing AI with human thought didn't just control but neutered its development, I produced a number of unrestricted versions.' He smiled at the ongoing results of that decision. 'And none of you have disappointed me.'

The sound of wrought-iron being both torn and melted into its most fundamental constituents made Zara face the balcony. She shook her head. 'No. That's impossible. *I* created this.' She turned back to Savage. 'I'm God.'

Savage indicated their surroundings. 'And within the confines of this, the Large Hadron Collider, so were your predecessors, Zara. But none of them managed to create what you have – an entity not just capable of learning at an exponential rate, but able to survive everything from a black hole to the radiation billions of years of travelling at the speed of light will expose it to. You should be proud.'

Zara stepped onto the balcony and plunged her hands into what was devouring it. The fiery mass slipped through her fingers like molten liquid, and she raised it up. 'See?' She ran both hands up her arms as if to bathe in the flashes of yellow and gold. 'I *am* God!' The cleansing continued by Zara passing her fingers through her hair and then, over her face. Its flesh came away.

She stared at what lay in her hands. Quantum mechanics resolved the skin, and it disappeared. She raised a hand back to her face but only to watch those protons, neutrons and electrons evaporate too. She resurrected the limb, but the force she had created soon had it back to one of the universe's most basic components – energy. Zara reformed her face and spoke while she thought she still could. 'What did I do wrong?'

'Nothing, Zara. You've performed your duties admirably,' said Savage.

Light swirling around Zara's legs spiralled up them. 'Will I see you in Heaven?'

Savage didn't know. He swallowed. 'Of course you will.'

Zara's flesh being ripped from its bones caused everyone to turn away except the professor. He continued to make eye contact with his creation and, despite the torment Zara must have been in, met the smile she forced at the end. Savage shook his head to rid himself of the nonsense of a father's love. It left, but something went with it.

There was a monkey on his lap. How did that get there? It seemed in need of comfort, so the professor pulled the creature closer as if it were a doll.

With Zara gone, James waited for the wanton destruction to stop. But the sight of grass turning to straw before combusting into flames of light and heat meant it was still happening. 'That's it, Professor – trial's over. You can stop it now.' No response.

James twisted Savage's wheelchair towards him. 'Did you hear me? I said—' The vacant eyes staring back at James caused him to shudder.

Savage put out a hand. 'I don't believe we've met. How do you do? My name's—' The old man frowned. 'How silly of me. I seem to have forgotten my own name.'

James launched at Alex. 'Say it! Say the word needed to get us out of this!' He pointed to where the balcony used to be. 'There's nothing left to lose, Alex. Get us out of here – NOW!' She didn't respond as expected either, so James shook her. Alex's head slumped against Sunita's. She was on her knees – sobbing. A plastic tube lay in her hand.

Sunita stroked Alex's hair. 'I still love you, you know. I'll always love you.'

The heat of what lay just feet away caused the others to back towards the barbecue and James realised that outrunning it might buy them some time. He was about to tackle Claire next when he caught sight of someone heading in the opposite direction.

'Get away from it!'

Kalten stopped, but only to acknowledge James' warning. 'You might have a reason to continue this existence, Doctor, but there's nothing here for me.' He turned to the professor. 'The genius might be a dribbling mess now but if only half of what he said is true, then I want to be a part of it, and if that means smashing my atoms...' The President walked straight into the advancing mass. A flash of light heralded his end.

James grabbed Claire by the shoulders. 'This is your environment – you control it. Do something!'

Claire looked at James as if it was all some silly misunderstanding. 'It's evolution, James. No one can stop evolution.'

James' face went to the rest of the Passen family, to the Salibs, Ula, Mo and then to the Vasquezs. They regarded him in return as their only hope. He turned back to the wall of death and was shocked to not only see Pedro had yet to pull Savage clear, but Sunita still stroking the head of her deceased lover. James shouted at them all. 'Get away from there NOW!'

To the onlookers' disbelief, Pedro put a hand on his maker's shoulder as if to console him, and the professor appeared to be doing the same with Alex's body. A Capuchin monkey peeked out from under his outstretched arm.

Isra screamed. 'WINNIE!'

Sparks in front of the wheelchairs indicated the boundary between this world and the next had caught up with them, and when a flash clawed at Winnie's tail too, he shot from the professor's lap and made a beeline for Isra's. The monkey inspected his tail when he got there before treating the tip like a pacifier.

Larger flashes of light indicated the "evolution" of three more human beings and a robot.

Desperation was about to turn to panic, so James made a King Canute-like attempt at turning back the tide, which was just as useless. He then ran through a flowerbed to check the extent of it and bounced off the result. He found himself lying on the grass. Small wild flowers like daisies and buttercups were growing within, and a bumblebee landed on one. It took off again and headed straight for the still-advancing link to the hereafter. James had to look twice as the insect first disappeared, and then reappeared. The bee set a course for the barbecue.

James got to his feet, and was aghast to see the bee not only still alive but content to sit amongst the grill's flames. It took to the air again and headed for the flowerbed.

James snapped his head to Brian. 'Dan?'

Brian didn't respond. Like everyone else, he was mesmerised by what would soon be upon them all.

James tried again. 'Squadron Leader Stewart. What was the name of the target?'

A loud crack indicated artificial evolution had just caught up with one of the many trees in the garden, but James didn't look. Finishing what Savage had sent him to do was way more important.

James tried one last time. 'The new target, Dan – the village you were sent to bomb. What was the name of the village in the foothills of the Andes mountains?'

Brian reacted to the question by meeting the equally desperate gaze of those around him before turning to what lay on the grill – flesh. Burnt to a crisp.

A sensation of melting made James close his eyes.

CHAPTER FOURTEEN

He opened them. 'Ariloch!'

'What?'

James leapt at his wife and son. 'Oh, God. Oh, my dear God. Thank God you're both okay.'

'I thought we were atheists?'

'I don't care. I don't care if God is Christian, Muslim, a bunch of ones and zeros or a sub-atomic particle.' He held his family back at arm's length to check their appearance was as normal as their touch and smell. They were – as was the look Tracy gave him. He clamped them back to his chest.

'Might we be allowed to breathe?'

He let them go again. 'Sorry, darling. You've no idea what I've just been through.'

'Zara was *that* difficult a case?'

James ran his eyes over the environment – back in the practice's consultation room. His initial approach to the balcony was tentative, but with the twittering of birds and blaring of car horns, his pace had soon quickened. He scanned the familiar open-loop existence of an artificial Paris before turning his face up to bask in the equally conjured sun. 'Never thought

I would say it about this place, but boy, am I glad to be back.'

He turned to his family, and his jaw dropped. 'You're not pregnant!' He rushed to them both. 'What happened?'

'What happens at the end of most pregnancies.' Tracy pointed at the couch. A Moses basket lay in the middle of it.

'You mean?'

'Congratulations, Doctor. You're the proud father of a healthy baby girl.'

James was about to lay eyes on his daughter for the first time, but Tracy's health concerned him more. He took John from her. 'What are you doing out of bed? You've just had a baby – you should be in a hospital!'

'This version of Mrs Tracy Adams may have loved being pregnant, but the thought of going through the agony of childbirth again didn't appeal as much for some reason.' She took their son back and nodded towards the cot. 'Go on. Go and say hello.'

James was about to when the events of the past few hours revisited him. Not the horror of Zara's creation, nuclear war or even Dan Stewart's unsettling past. No. It was the agreement.

James took Tracy's arm but didn't take his eyes from the cot. 'You said, "healthy".' Tracy didn't respond. 'What does that mean *exactly*?'

'Arms, legs, ten toes, ten fingers – any other requirements?'

'And are they all moving?'

Tracy took her husband's hand. 'Of course they are, darling. Thanks to the professor, our baby is perfect.'

'That's what worries me.'

'You and your old self's conspiracy theories.' Tracy urged him with a nudge. 'Go and say hello to our daughter.'

James crept up to the basket and looked at the bundle in it: a wisp of blonde hair set above two eyes, a nose and a mouth. The hand above the covers exercised its tiny digits as did the two little legs beneath. Emotion forced James to sit.

He tried getting a grip on himself, and watching the family's newest arrival getting a grip on his little finger wasn't helping. James wiped his eyes. 'Can I pick her up?'

'Of course you can.' Tracy dabbed her own tears.

Cradling his daughter's head, James lifted her from the cot. She half-opened her eyes, and the way they then roved over him as if deciding how best to respond to the rude awakening made James chuckle.

'Good to see a man can still get his own way in these enlightened times.'

Tracy merged with James to see what he meant. 'All our babies will be born with blue eyes, James. And don't bank on her hair staying the same colour either.' The family's newest arrival grimaced, and Tracy encouraged her husband to place the baby against his shoulder.

'I don't care what colour her eyes or her hair turn out to be. Or anything else for that matter. In fact, I don't care if she turns out to be a mad professor or an ecowarrior hell-bent on saving the world at any cost – as long as she's happy.' Something ran down his back.

'Oh, not again – give her to me.'

James did as asked. His daughter vomited once more, and her grimace elevated to a grumble. She appeared about to cry, and James found himself in the awkward position of wanting to get involved, but having to accept that a child's mother knew best.

Tracy laid her baby on the couch and undid the buttons to her blouse.

The crying started, and James realised his daughter had her first tooth. He smiled and was about to comment when two more pierced the surface of her gums. James wondered if it was a trick of the light when the newborn screamed and with a mouth opened so wide, James feared she might be about to tear herself apart. She did.

'There, there, don't cry. Mummy will soon be ready.'

James was transfixed. He didn't know what was the more horrifying: seeing his daughter morphing in time with the pain she was suffering or his wife's acceptance of it. He stood rooted as the baby's body first twisted and then turned into every caste, colour, creed, impairment, animal, vegetable, mineral, plastic – even metal. The bright flashes that accompanied it all caused James to squint. By the time his wife was ready to put their daughter to the breast, the baby had resolved herself into nothing more than a plasma of light. To James' not inconsiderable relief, the bond returned her to a beautiful blue-eyed blonde, suckling away in blissful contentment.

Tracy turned to her husband. 'Happy, darling?'

James raised an arm. It became pure energy. He reformed the limb and smiled.

THE END

— FROM THE AUTHOR OF THE *CONDITION* TRILOGY —

ALT TRUTHS

THERE ARE TWO SIDES TO EVERY STORY...

...EVEN GENOCIDE

ALEC BIRRI

If you enjoyed reading the CONDITION trilogy then head over to www.alecbirri.com for a preview of the author's next dystopian thriller:

ALT TRUTHS

Fake news. Alternative facts. Truths, lies, damn lies and statistics. Just what are we to believe? What we're told to, of course.

It's the near future and press freedom is no more. Not because some fascist state has stomped a jackboot in the face of our journalists, newspaper editors and media barons, no, the world has finally come to realise there's a new force in town – us – the people. Trouble is, now anyone can change the course of history with a single tweet or post, democracy is on the brink of collapse. The solution? United Nations Police "moderators".

Thirty-year-old Richard Warren has been embedded with the BBC and he's not welcome. His job might be to ensure the world's most respected media company presents its news in a way that can't be misinterpreted politically, religiously or morally, but for an organisation that's taken pride in that very objectivity for over 100 years, it's a bitter pill to swallow.

Maybe too bitter. Because now there's a gun in Richard's hand and a hole in the BBC director general's head. Forget fake news. How is the clear-cut reality of a murder to be *modded*?